Snowflakes for an Earl

Christmas Wallflowers

Sandra Sookoo

New Independence Books

SNOWFLAKES FOR AN EARL © 2022 by Sandra Sookoo
Published by New Independence Books

ISBN- 9798358381056

Contact Information:
sandrasookoo@yahoo.com
newindependencebooks@gmail.com
Visit me at www.sandrasookoo.com

Book Cover Design by Victoria Miller

Publishing History:
First Print Edition, 2022

Dear Readers,

Every year, I have a few readers who request a sweet Christmas romance. This book is that, and because of the word count restraint, I felt there wasn't time for a sexy times scene anyway.

Also, for the purposes of this story, when I make mention of the moons of Mars, bear in mind that popular opinion states these moons weren't "discovered" until the 1850s. However, I am of the opinion that amateur astronomers could have discovered/seen these moons, as well as theorized that each planet has moons, earlier in the century. Just because the "discoveries" are notated in official papers didn't mean they hadn't happened.

I hope you enjoy this couple! The story ended up being a cute, romantic read.

Sandra

Dedication

To Christina Lorenzen. Thanks for your support over the years and for loving my stories. It makes all the difference.

Blurb

At times, believing is more important than seeing in matters of love and snowflakes.

It's Christmastide 1817 and Miss Christiana Smythe, daughter of a squire, is not looking forward to the social obligations of the season. Wanting nothing more than to care for the area's sick and ailing animal population, doing the rounds in glittering ballrooms festooned with holiday finery makes her lightheaded. Yet it's a necessity to realizing the dream of love.

Evan Tennant, Earl of Stanton's priorities are to avoid dancing with women he doesn't know as well as to evade match-making mamas. He'd much rather spend his time charting the stars in the hopes of catching a meteor shower, yet he has responsibilities to his title and his mother insists he find an eligible lady soon. Except he doesn't believe in romance or the magic of Christmastide.

Though she's a confirmed wallflower, Christiana's knack for helping animals throws her into the earl's path when his beloved beagle falls ill. Attraction as hot and bright as a comet's tail takes them both by surprise. Through a series of odd events, they're thrown together, and when kisses and dances edge them closer to love, they'll both need a little push before they believe what fate knew all along.

Chapter One

December 20, 1817
Chatham Cottage
Derbyshire, England

Miss Christiana Smythe prowled through the barn while lifting her lantern high. Yesterday, she'd stumbled upon a mother beagle who'd made herself a den in one of the stalls and had birthed seven little puppies. Now, she wanted to check on the health of all the dogs and make certain the babies were doing well.

"There you are." The golden illumination flooded the straw in the stall where the mother dog lay. Six puppies reclined haphazardly, laying into her side, all asleep. One puppy was off to the side, and Christiana could already tell it hadn't lasted through the night. "How are you?" Thankfully, it wasn't frigid cold, so the dogs should fare well enough. She hung the lantern on a hook on the side of the barn. "How's the new mother?"

After she knelt on the straw nearby, a quick check on the one puppy confirmed that it had indeed expired. With a sigh, she draped one of the old blankets she'd brought over the pup and would dispose of it later. The other blanket she tucked around the mother and some of the squirming pups. "It looks like your family is hale and hearty for the most part." Methodically, Christiana picked up each of the puppies, gave them a cursory examination before returning them to the mother's side. "Quite a handsome litter you had, Bess."

The mother beagle looked at her with tired but pleased eyes. A soft woof was the dog's answer, and Christiana smiled.

"I imagine you *are* exhausted," she crooned to the dog. She patted the mother's sleek brown and white head, smiled when two of the puppies snuggled closer to their mother. "You take care of them, and I shall take care of you."

In all her five and twenty years, there was never anything else Christiana aspired to beyond working with animals. There had always been a certain affinity for them since her first memories. Whether nurturing them, caring for them, helping them grow, healing them when they were sick or injured, she was at her most happy when surrounded by living things with fur or the occasional feather. Now that she had matured into an adult, everyone on the estate knew if there was trauma with one of their animals, they'd do well to bring it to her attention first.

Once the mother beagle drifted off to sleep, Christiana stood and moved across the aisle to one of the other stalls. The horse within had recently been cut by some thorns when it ran afoul of a briar patch on the property.

"Hullo, Moonlight." Named for her blonde coat that shimmered as if she were moonlight personified, the mare was a gorgeous creature. "How are you feeling this evening?" She moved to the horse's left side, smoothed her palms along the soft neck to the belly where the bulk of the scratches had marred and snagged the flesh.

A soft wuffle came from the horse with the slight dip of her head.

"It looks like the cuts are healing nicely." Thanks in large part to the salve she'd slathered onto the jagged injuries. It was of her own compounding, which she did in the still room nearby. They'd scabbed over and had shrunk. In a day or two, they would be hardly noticeable. "That is nice to see."

"Yer doin' God's work here, Miss Smythe," one of the grooms said as he entered the barn to deposit a saddle on the side of one of the stalls.

She recognized it as belonging to her brother, who was the squire and had been since their father had died five years before of gout.

That meant Thomas had returned from his customary evening ride. "I don't like seeing any living being in pain or suffering."

"England needs more hearts like yours, miss. Not everyone has your gifts." Once another of the grooms led her brother's horse into the barn and then the stall, the first groom took a brush in hand in readiness to give the equine his nightly once over.

Before she could retrieve her lantern, Thomas entered.

"Ah, I somehow thought you would be here, Sis." He was the squire of the area, but he also served as the local magistrate, which surprisingly kept him busy.

"It's part of my nightly rounds." She flashed a smile at her only sibling. Since their mother had died in childbirth fifteen years before and their father more recently, Thomas was one of a few living relatives. A cousin and her son lived in London. "The pups are doing well."

Her brother nodded. "Once they're weaned, I imagine we won't have trouble finding homes for them."

"*Most* of them." She glanced back at the stall. "There are a couple of pups I'll wish to keep." They were all adorable, but the black and brown ones were her favorites.

"Of course." He uttered a snort while scratching his gloved fingers through his dark brown hair so much like her own. In another few years, if he didn't cease eating rich foods, he would follow in their father's footsteps. "At least they'll prove good hunters if their mother is any indication."

"Perhaps." She stood at the stall door and watched the dogs for a few minutes. "Did you have a lovely ride tonight?"

"I did. Fortunately, it's not raining, but I fear we'll have all too much of that in the coming days."

"Unless it grows colder. I still haven't given up hope it will snow for Christmas." She turned about, gently closed the door and then leaned her back against it. "Why do I have the feeling you aren't here to talk about the weather with me?"

"Because I'm not. Something has been on my mind of late." He crossed his arms at his chest, leaned a shoulder against a post between stalls, and then sighed. "Listen, you really need to move on with the business of finding a husband."

Ah, so then there was the truth of it, and it was a conversation they had a few times a year. "Why? Do you wish me out from underfoot?" It wasn't as if her brother entertained all that much, thank the stars. She felt uncomfortable enough in society.

"Well, yes." A flush rose over his collar. "I cannot go up to London and perhaps entice a lady to marry me while I still have the responsibility of you. My loyalties are split, but it's rather time for me to make something of myself and leave a legacy."

At least he was taking responsibility. "While that's all well and good, I am quite content with my lot." She pointed her eyes heavenward at the absurdity of his request. "I have the animals to care for, and it's good work."

"It's noble enough, sure, but a young lady such as yourself is being wasted here in the country." Thomas drew his fingers through his hair. "Besides, you're growing long in the tooth as we speak."

"Ah. Since when is five and twenty ancient?"

"It's not, of course, but for the Marriage Mart, it means you're nearly expired."

The very idea of putting herself on display for various bachelors, widowers, or men seeking a mother for their children sent a chill down her spine. So much so that Christiana huffed. "You know the ordeal of doing the pretty in society makes me ill." There had been times in her life where she'd cast up her accounts in a lady's retiring room at a ball.

"Yes, well, since it's rather unlikely some well-to-do nob is going to swoop down here on this property and catch your eye, you are going to have to put yourself into positions where that might be possible." Thomas shrugged. His expression indicated he'd had enough of the argument. "If you cannot find a suitable man in the country, I'll be forced to rent a townhouse in Town after Twelfth Night and hopefully find a sponsor to help see you launched. That sort of expense will put a rather large dent in our coffers, which I need for spring repairs."

Oh, dear. Worry knotted in her belly. "I am well past the age of being launched."

"That would mean you have already done such a thing," he shot off with a snicker.

Another huff of annoyance escaped her. "You know what I mean, and you also know that the eligible candidates around the area are enough to make anyone shudder." Christiana frowned. "I never aspired to be any man's wife." In fact, she still didn't, yet in order to meet a secret dream she'd carried, she would have to.

"While that is all true, something must be done. A man simply isn't going to appear here as if by magic and become enchanted by you." When she would have given him a tart rebuttal, he held up a hand. "So, as an answer to the conundrum, you are going to attend the Earl of Stanton's annual Christmas Eve ball."

Oh, my stars! The Earl of Stanton was their nearest neighbor in the country. His estate butted against her brother's. Rarely did their social circles overlap, and as titled gentlemen went, he was rather young to hold the position.

Rarely had she seen him about the area. The feeling of wishing to be sick climbed her throat. "Must I?" The event was held every year without fail, whether the earl was in the country or not.

"I am afraid you must." He lifted an eyebrow. "Life is too short to spend it alone, and you'll make some man a good wife."

And thus, she'd been neatly confined into the small parameters allowed women in this age. "As if that is the only destiny I have before me?" Yet if she wished to realize the dream of becoming a mother, she had no choice except to marry. "No one ever thinks women are capable of becoming more than some man's wife or some child's mother." It was a statement of fact. Then she gestured to the dogs and included the horses in her regard. "What of my hopes to open some sort of a clinic to care for injured animals?" For years, that wish had superseded becoming a mother. "There is a great need for such in our community." She dreamed about it regularly. "We could convert one of the outbuildings with a couple of examination tables, some cages if the animals need to be under overnight observation, and medical supplies."

"Hell's bells, Christiana. Animals won't care for you in old age."

"Perhaps not." With a last lingering glance at the beagles, she sighed. "But they *can* bring me comfort and happiness. Isn't that more important? And what if you marry me off to a detestable man who beats me or ignores me? At least my animals will give me the love my union might lack."

And the possibility of that terrified her. In all the years her parents had been married, they'd enjoyed love and laughter into their middle age. She wanted the same, but the likelihood of that happening with the current pool of men didn't seem possible, especially when she was nothing more than a wallflower when it came to social outings.

"I think I'm rather more reliable than marrying you to a bounder." Her brother snorted. "Animals cannot give you the children you want."

"Perhaps not." Heat slapped at her cheeks. "However, animals *could* be considered children…"

"Come off it, Christiana." Thomas leveled a look on her that brooked no arguments. "You're going to the Christmas Eve ball. Best square with it now, for I want you married by May Day, so I can finally start my own life."

"A life that doesn't include me, your own sister?" The knowledge hit her more intensely than she'd anticipated. "You are my only close family, Thomas."

He visibly crumbled. "I won't throw you to the wolves. I promise." When he bundled her into his arms and hugged her, her eyebrows soared in surprise, for he wasn't a demonstrative man. That was something he'd inherited from their father. "I shall make certain the man you marry is a good sort."

"Yet you still wish for me to wed," she whispered, and rapidly blinked away the tears that sprang to her eyes as she pulled out of his arms.

"It's for the best, and once you think about it, you will realize I'm correct."

She rather doubted it. "I can keep house for you."

"No. I want you to have your own life, not exist on the perimeter of mine." He patted her cheek. "In this, I won't budge. Now, come inside. No doubt dinner will be served soon." Without another word, he left the barn.

A sigh left her throat. When she caught one of the groom's eyes, she shrugged. "Ah, Sam. Why can my brother not understand I am better as a wallflower, that I'm most comfortable staying off a dance floor and out of drawing rooms? That there is nothing wrong with not marrying?" There was no shame in admitting to that fact; most of the staff knew it.

"I can't say as I understand it much myself, miss." The older groom shrugged. "I'd marry you if Sir Smythe would let me."

He was such a dear, and she'd known him since she was old enough to speak. Christiana smiled. "It is a lovely thought. Thank you." And the man was at least twenty years her senior. "I shall bear that in mind in the event I need a plan to fall back on."

"Just say the word, miss." Then he returned to putting clean straw in the stall.

With her thoughts decidedly taking a downward spiral, Christiana retrieved her lantern and then slowly made her way out of the barn. There were four days before the ball, and truly, she had nothing fancy to wear to such an elevated society event. A visit to a modiste's shop in the village was in order, and since her brother was the one pushing for this, he could receive the bill later in the month.

God help us both.

Chapter Two

December 20, 1817
Stanton Hall
Derbyshire, England

The clink of silverware against china echoed in the nearly empty dining room. Evan Tennant, 10th Earl of Stanton, held his cut crystal wine glass so tight he feared he would break it with the slightest more pressure.

His patience finally snapped. Better it than the stemware. "Damnation, Mother, could we *please* talk about something — anything — else?"

In the corner, curled in a large willow basket lined with old pillows, his beagle George whined and followed it up with a preemptory bark. No doubt the dog could sense his distress and wished to provide protection.

For the last thirty minutes, through the first two courses of dinner, his parent had mapped out plans to have him wed by summer. Plans that went against everything he stood for in his life, for he'd been engaged ten years before as a young man of twenty. Perhaps he'd been brash and stupid, but he'd fallen tip over tail after interacting with a chit only twice. Their engagement was immediate and short, for neither of them had wished to delay a nuptial ceremony. Except his dear Melissa had expired that winter ten days before the wedding of an ailment of the lungs. It had been a particularly hard, cold snap wherein she'd caught a head cold that had taken up residence in her lungs; nothing could save her.

That had been on Christmas Eve and had also been when the magic of life had died for him. He'd loved her to distraction, and all of his dreams had died with her. Nothing had been the same since, certainly not the state of his heart.

"Language, Evan," his mother tsked without glancing up from her plate. "You were raised better than that."

"I was, but when you constantly ignore my wishes, you must know my annoyance flares and I cannot be held responsible for what I say." As gently as he could, Evan set his wineglass down. His appetite had fled, and the creamed chicken soup no longer appealed. "In answer to your original subject matter, I am adamant I do *not* need to marry."

She heaved out a sigh and finally focused her blue gaze on him. "Dearest, we have been over the whys and wherefore *ad nauseum*." No matter that she was five and fifty, she still retained many of the looks she'd had in his childhood, though silver strands wove through her blonde tresses, and more than a few wrinkles gave her once-smooth face character. Though she'd borne three children, Evan was the only one who'd survived into adulthood. "You must make inroads into begetting an heir."

He huffed out his frustration. "There is time yet for that. I'm not yet ancient."

"Your father started his nursery much earlier than this."

"Different times, Mother."

Calmly, as if she wasn't aware she ruffled his proverbial feathers, his mother took several spoonfuls of her soup. "If you don't find yourself a suitable lady, I will have to do it for you."

Oh, dear lord. "You are aware I have attained my thirtieth year and am responsible for navigating my own life? That I've done rather well for myself since Father died?" His chest tightened, for that loss was only two years old and still not far enough in the past that it didn't cease to hurt. "I don't require a nursemaid or governess, and I certainly don't need my mother to be led by the hand."

The corners of her mouth twitched with the beginnings of a smile that never materialized. "And you are aware none of us live forever?" One of her blonde eyebrows rose. "Time is of the essence, Stanton. Marry and get a woman breeding. At least until you have your heir. Then you may do what you please."

"There is a jot more to it than that." He couldn't keep the sarcasm from his voice. Where he'd meant to live the remainder of his life married to Melissa, fate had other plans.

How could he offer up his heart to possibly be broken like that again?

The beagle in its bed whined, which recalled Evan's attention to the animal himself. He'd meant to give his fiancée the beagle as a puppy for a Christmas gift the year she'd died, but now he had had George for ten years, and though he loved the canine, it was sometimes painful for him to remember constantly.

"I rather think there isn't." When she caught the eye of a footman and gestured to the table, the young man sprang into action clearing the dishes in preparation for the next course. "I have no grandchildren. Why does my only child hate me so much to withhold such joy?"

"You know that's not true."

"Do I? You need to do your duty by the title. And that means marrying well."

"Because, heaven forbid, I marry beneath my station merely to see it done?" He couldn't resist shooting off the comment. "And you well know why I'm reluctant to marry."

"Pish posh. You have no more time to trot out the excuse of a broken heart. Enough time has passed to heal and move forward, and you well know it." She shook a finger at him while the footman put a plate of roasted pheasant in front of her. "No sense in living alone when there is no need, and since you just returned to the country, there is no time to lose."

"You seem to have everything well in hand with ball preparations." Evan had spent much of the year in Town, for the parliament season had been a busy one, and the last thing he'd wished to do was return to his country estate and allow memories to deluge him. This time of the year had been difficult since losing Melissa, and though those feelings had faded as the years marched on, he certainly wasn't interested in marrying.

Of course, he'd taken lovers for he wasn't a monk, but none of those women had captivated him or prompted him to offer an engagement. He'd never connected with them on the same level he had with Melissa. However, perhaps he was a paradox of sorts, for he did enjoy spending Christmastide at Stanton Hall and hosting his annual Christmas Eve ball in his father's tradition. There was always a peace inherent in the country one couldn't find in London, which let him study the stars in the night sky with ease, but the ball was always marred by matchmaking mamas throwing their daughters at him. To say nothing of available widows.

And now his own mother with her demands that he marry and provide an heir.

Truly, it was a mess that brought naught but wasted time.

"Of course I do. The ball is an annual event." His mother cut into her pheasant while he did the same. "Because you are an eligible, titled lord, that alone will draw a crush."

A long-suffering sigh escaped him. "How lovely for you." The fly in the ointment was the fact his mother was right. His father had died of a stroke, so he really should set his affairs in order in the event he suffered the same health woes. "Fine. You win. I grow weary of arguing." After shoveling in a forkful of food and chewing furiously, he swallowed. "I shall go into this week with marriage in mind and will search diligently over the ladies present at the ball for countess material."

"I am happy to hear it." For the first time since the meal started, his mother smiled. "It will be nice to have another woman about."

"And you to move into the dower house? Obviously, if I marry, you will be the dowager and certainly not the mistress around here." When she narrowed her eyes, he stood and threw his linen napkin to the tabletop. "Now, if you'll excuse me, I'm going out to chart the stars." It's where he felt most comfortable.

"You haven't finished your dinner."

"My appetite has fled in any event. The stars are more thrilling." For as long as he could remember, he'd been fascinated with the stars and the constellations. To say nothing of the planets.

She frowned. "Whyever do you wish to be outside? There is a decided chill in the air."

"Studying the stars is fascinating to me. There's a chance I'll be able to see the Geminids meteor shower if the damned rain holds off this week." It didn't happen often, but the if the conditions were right over the next week, he could catch part of the phenomena. "Can you imagine seeing blazes of fire as bits of space fall through the air to the earth?"

"I can honestly say I have never imagined that."

"If I'm fortunate, I might spy a planet or two tonight." Then he warmed to his subject. "Venus was named for the Roman goddess of beauty, love, fertility, prosperity, and desire. Mars was named after the Roman god of war and agriculture."

"What does this have anything to do with the current subject?" A trace of annoyance rode his mother's inquiry.

"I'm coming to it. According to one version of this tale, Venus was married to Vulcan, the god of fire, but she fell in love with Mars."

"Too bad I'm not his mother," she muttered before taking a sip of wine.

Evan rolled his eyes. "In any event, Venus had many children with Mars, including Phobos—which means fear—and Deimos—which means terror. Those are the names of the moons of Mars."

"Even the god managed to have children. What do you not understand about this?"

"Mother, you are clearly missing the point." He shook his head. Sometimes, there was no understanding. "These moons might be asteroids trapped in the planet's gravitational pull. I suppose we won't know for certain until we can see them. Mars and Venus often appear close together in our sky at that time, and perhaps that is why the Romans named them 'wandering stars' after those two lovers."

"Lovers who are only myths." His mother leveled a look upon him. "Don't make your love life become the same."

"I won't, of course, but I cannot rush love and romance."

"You can if the union is arranged." She laid her fork down on her plate. "You might think all of this a joke, but I do not. Your attention should be on the Marriage Mart and not on the stars."

He shook his head. "A man can be interested in two things at once."

"Yet you are drawn to the heavens." She blew out a breath. "Whether you like it or not, you are an earl. You have responsibilities and duty, a position to maintain within the *ton*. And you are thirty. It is long past time for you to stop mooning about over the memory of a dead girl and work with what is in front of you."

"In which case, there are no women in front of me until they all decide to trip on their damned hems in the ballroom in four days!" His words echoed off the walls.

"Evan, please. Some decorum."

"No. I am done letting you harangue me about marriage as if I don't have an opinion." The remainder of his patience snapped. "Melissa was the first woman I ever loved. You hated her then and apparently still do. I cannot easily dismiss the hurt her death brought."

"You can and you will, Stanton. Ten years is past time to cycle through mourning." Her voice became more shrill. "You need a wife, and eligible women aren't found in the stars! During the upcoming Christmastide holidays, you will center your attention on social events and that's that."

He tamped the urge to grin, for it was quite personally rewarding to see his mother fly into the boughs. "More's the pity, for there are plenty of romantic stories set there that would make any man believe in the power of love."

Except, he didn't. Not since his fiancée had passed, and he probably wouldn't ever again.

"But I did make you a promise, so I will keep it." He whistled for the dog, who bounded to his feet with alacrity. "Come, boy."

Such was life, and if that meant he was stunted emotionally or with his mental faculties, so be it. Evan didn't much care, and he certainly didn't give it another thought as he strode through the corridors and then stormed outside.

Since he didn't have his telescope with him, staring at the skies with his naked eye would have to do, for he didn't wish to spare the time returning to the house. As soon as he was far enough away from the house's illumination and on the back lawn, he stopped with his hands upon his hips. "What the hell should I do, George?" Recently, he'd taken to talking to his dog as if the beagle would respond with words.

With a sharp bark, the canine sat on the ground at Evan's feet. He placed a paw on the toe of his boot.

"I know, there are things I must attend to in my life, but I am fearful of loving someone so fiercely I might be hurt again." Perhaps it was good to admit that to a living being who couldn't run off and repeat the words.

A soft woof was the only answer.

"Take a chance?" He snorted. "On whom? There are hardly women about I would consider good enough for a countess." Would the Christmas Eve ball bring more variety? When he glanced down at the dog, he sighed. "Perhaps I should put that decision into your paws, George. I'll wager you'd have better luck in the matchmaking arena than my mother."

God help us all.

Chapter Three

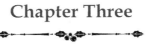

December 21, 1817
Chatham Cottage
Derbyshire, England

Christiana turned another page in the novel she was reading. While it was a gripping tale of unrequited love and danger, it didn't truly hold her attention, for she would much rather be out in the barn with the new puppies. Yet at the back of her mind was the worry of attending the Earl of Stanton's Christmas Eve ball in three days.

She laid down her book as knots of anxiety pulled in her belly. Earlier that day she'd gone into the village and spoke with a seamstress at the dressmaker's shop. Thankfully, a client had cancelled a finished order, so she was able to purchase that dress and have it altered, so the expense of finding a suitable gown hadn't been extreme. Still, if she could do anything else besides attending a social function, she would.

Drat Thomas and his dictate that she marry! She wasn't fundamentally opposed to the wedded state—as long as the man in question let her chase her own dreams—but why did meeting men need to come on the heels of attending society events and putting herself on display as if she were horseflesh at auction?

Several minutes later, a commotion drifted to her ears, followed by a sharp bark of a dog and then a whine from that same animal. "What is happening?" She launched to her feet, and the book tumbled unheeded to the Aubusson carpet. Since her brother had business in the village, she would take command of whatever the situation required.

Once Christiana gained the ground floor, the butler led a rather handsome man with an older beagle in his arms along the corridor then into the parlor. The man's face showed signs of strain, but for what? And why had he brought a beagle into the house?

"What is amiss, Matthews?" she asked of the butler who saw the visitor settled before turning to face her.

"The Earl of Stanton is here to ask for your assistance."

"What?" As shock barreled through her chest, Christiana glanced at the man who talked softly to the beagle in his lap. "*He* is the earl?" The whisper sounded overly loud in the sudden hush of the room. She'd never had cause to meet

His Lordship, especially since he'd come into the title. For that matter, she'd only met his father once, a handful of years ago, when he'd visited her parents for tea.

Despite the rumors that held the earl hadn't much in the way of looks, that he was a man easily forgotten once the conversation ended, he was definitely attractive to her. Thick, blond hair done into the latest style similar to what her brother preferred, full eyebrows of the same hue, strong, aristocratic features that proclaimed him of the upper class, but he wasn't an Adonis by any stretch. Neither did he possess arresting lines, but there was *something* about him that caused her pulse to flutter. Perhaps it was the fact he held a dog in his arms.

The man in question cleared his throat. "I am." He rose up from the sofa, and good heavens, he was as tall as her brother. Since she stood at just over two inches over five feet, they were perhaps both eight inches above her height. "Forgive me for the intrusion, but there was simply no time for pleasantries. I'm the Earl of Stanton, and this," he gestured at the dog in his arms with his chin, "is George."

"He is quite a nice-looking beagle." All sleek brown and black fur, but there was marked pain in his big brown eyes and a few gray whiskers on his muzzle. "What seems to be the trouble?"

"This fellow took a tumble out of an upstairs window while one of the maids was airing bed linens." Sadness and panic flitted through the earl's expression. "It is possible George has a broken leg. And he has a nasty cut." He was obviously worried, for his voice was thick with strain. "One of my grooms suggested coming here because a Miss Smythe has an affinity and talent for nursing injured or unhealthy animals."

"Oh!" She looked at the butler, who gave her an encouraging nod. Warm pleasure went through her chest to know her reputation as a healer had circulated through the neighborhood and surrounding areas. Coming forward a few steps, Christiana looked at the earl. "I am Miss Smythe."

"Pleased to make your acquaintance." Then he sat on the sofa when the beagle began to squirm. "Pardon my lack of manners. He's rather heavy and I don't want him getting away."

"Understandable." Once more, she regarded the butler. "Matthews, please procure a pot of hot water, rags, and my sewing kit. Oh, and perhaps a stick or piece of wood I can use for a splint if needed."

"Of course, Miss Smythe." Once the butler departed the room, Christiana sighed.

"Do you mind if I examine the patient?"

"I would very much appreciate it, which is why I'm here." He shifted on the sofa so that the dog lay draped over his legs that were clad in ivory breeches. "I'm worried he might expire." When he lifted a hand and raked his fingers through his hair, she couldn't help but admire the breadth of his shoulders and chest highlighted by a jacket of dark blue superfine. His collar points weren't too high and his cravat not as starched nor arranged in an intricate knot, which made him that much more approachable.

"Oh, I rather doubt that will be the case. His still has some spunk." Putting the earl from her mind, she focused the whole of her concentration on the beagle as she kneeled on the floor at Lord Stanton's feet. "In the event one of his legs *is* broken, keep a good hold on him. My examination might inadvertently hurt him."

"I understand." He peered into the beagle's face. "Hold as still as you can, George. This nice lady will help you."

Christiana chuckled. "I shall try." Scooting closer, she smoothed a hand along the dog's sleek side. "How old is he?"

"Ten years. I, uh," his swallow was audible, "have had him since he was a pup. He's growing older but I don't wish to lose him just yet."

"I see." There didn't seem to be broken ribs. The dog's eyes followed her every movement. "Please turn him over." Once the earl did exactly that, she again felt for broken bones. "His ribs are normal." Then she turned her attention to the beagle's front legs. "Hullo, George. Hasn't anyone ever told you that you are a beagle instead of a bird and thusly cannot fly?"

When the earl chuckled, the rumbling sound tickled through her chest. "Beagles are incredibly stubborn. I don't know if he was chasing the bed linens or a bird."

She nodded but her fingers trembled as she moved on to the dog's hind legs. "Oh dear." On the left leg, a two-inch cut marred the fur. When she felt the leg, there were no broken bones, but the muscles were tender, for the dog whined and tried to squirm out of the earl's arms. "I wonder where he received his wound."

"With George, it could have been anything." Worry creased the earl's brow as he glanced at her. "Do you think infection will set in?"

Before she could answer, the butler returned with the items she'd requested. "Will there be anything else, Miss Smythe?"

"I cannot imagine there will be, but perhaps you can bring tea in a half hour?"

"Of course." Matthews laid the supplies on a low table. "I'll see to it at once."

"Thank you." Once more, her attention landed on the dog. "To the best of my knowledge, I believe George here has sprained or torn the muscle in this leg. But I rather doubt infection will come from his cut. However, I'll need to give him a few stitches."

Again, the beagle whined. This time he tried to remove himself from the earl's lap, but Lord Stanton held him close.

"None of that, George. Miss Smythe will make you better." He glanced at Christiana. "Thank you for your time and caring."

The gratitude in those rich, brown eyes sent flutters into her lower belly. "You are most welcome, Your Lordship. I don't like to see an animal suffering." Oh, he smelled so good! Like the crisp, clean air in the dead of winter. "Let me grab some supplies." Quickly, she stood and crossed to where her sewing kit rested.

"Are stitches truly necessary?" Concern threaded through the earl's voice.

"Yes, because the cut is deep, and if I don't, the skin won't knit back together. That's when infection might set in." Christiana took up a folded rag and carefully wet it with some of the hot water. She returned to the dog, carefully washed the wound as best she could. After, she went back to the table where she traded the rag for the needle and thread, which she readied. Then she grabbed a bottle of brandy that had been included as well as the basket of supplies, and returned, once more kneeling before him and the dog. "If you are squeamish, I can ring for a footman."

The poor man *did* look a bit green about the gills. "I'm not leaving my dog."

"Good man." It spoke to his character. "This won't take long." After putting the basket on the floor beside her, she splashed a bit of the brandy over her needle, took up a rag and did the same with it. "Here. Perhaps this will do you some good as well." When she offered the earl the brandy, he accepted the bottle. As their fingers brushed, sweet heat danced up her arm. "Here we go," she said quickly into the silence. Only then did she press it against the wound. The dog yelped.

The earl petted the dog's head, but he did take a healthy swig of the brandy with his other hand. "Hold still, George."

While Christiana tended to the injury, she chattered on, to fill the silence as well to take the earl's mind off the handiwork. "Are you excited for the upcoming holiday and your annual ball?" Gently, she drew her needle through the dog's flesh and fur. It was essential to put the canine's whines to the back of her mind. "I'm told it is quite the event of the social season."

"While that might be true, I am *not* looking forward to it." There was such a decided note of distaste in his tones that she glanced up.

"Oh? I'm surprised. It's a tradition for your family."

He snorted. "Yes, well, that doesn't mean anything, does it?"

"I suppose not." Christiana quickly finished the stitches and tied off the thread. She sharply snipped it with her pair of sewing scissors. Then the needle and scissors went back into the sewing kit inside the basket. "The ball notwithstanding, don't you enjoy Christmastide?" She retrieved a clean rag and carefully wrapped it around the beagle's leg to cover his wound.

"Not particularly. The holiday reminds me of things I would rather forget." He took another sip of the brandy.

"I see." Even though she did not. As gently as she could, Christiana tied a bit of twine about the makeshift bandage in two places. "You will need to keep the dressing clean, but I will drop by for a visit tomorrow and put some salve on his wound."

"Thank you." Relief scudded across the earl's face. "Tell Miss Smythe thank you, George," he said to the dog.

George, to his credit, gave a soft woof and limply wagged his tail, but he slumped against the earl's chest. No doubt the canine was exhausted from his adventures.

"You are quite welcome." With a pat to the beagle's head, she stood, gathered her supplies into the basket as well as the brandy bottle, and then dropped everything into a nearby chair. With a sigh of relief, she smiled at the butler as he returned with the tea service. "Thank you, Matthews."

"Ring if you need anything else," he said on his way out of the room.

Without anything to serve as a distraction, Christiana sat on the sofa and reached for one of the delicate porcelain teacups. "Would you care for a cup, Lord Stanton?"

"Oh, yes, of course." Once the earl had carefully relocated the dog from his lap to the sofa cushion, he stood and then dropped into a chair near her location. "Thank you."

Again, when their fingers brushed as she gave him a cup, low grade heat went through her belly. That was slightly troubling, for she'd never had such a reaction to a man like that before. "Why do you not like Christmastide, if you don't mind me asking?"

He huffed out a breath. "I lost someone close to me days before Christmas years ago. This is a time when the memories haunt me." With gusto, he took a gulp of his tea. "Of course, much of my ire is from the fact that my mother wishes for me to marry, and she means to use the ball to stock the house with eligible women." A look of distaste crossed his face. "I would rather not fall victim to those machinations even if I have a responsibility to the title."

Her eyebrows rose. Why was he sharing such private details? Yes, she'd probably overstepped, but she was merely trying to make conversation and set him at ease. "Ah, you have had bad luck in that quarter. Of attracting women?"

"Not misfortune, but let's just say I don't wish to have my heart broken again." He frowned and stared into the depths of his teacup. "Is it that obvious?"

"A bit." She shrugged. "Perhaps I can sense it. Usually, such things happen to me with animals, but I suppose it works the same with people. But I do understand. I feel awkward in social situations."

"I see." Those sensuous lips of his turned downward in a frown as he looked at her.

Knowing she sounded like a ninny, she rushed onward. "Sometimes, though, in order for the duty and responsibility to go down more easily, you have to believe in the magic of romance, especially at this time of year."

"Ha!" The earl shook his head and then drained the remainder of his tea. "I will only believe in the magic of love and Christmastide if I see snowflakes fly by Christmas Eve."

"Oh." Christiana was lost in confusion. "It hasn't snowed in Derbyshire this early for ages." Usually, the snow held off until well after Twelfth Night.

His grin held no mirth. "Exactly." Swiftly, he stood and set his teacup on the table. "Thank you for the tea and for patching up my dog. I appreciate both, but now I must be off."

The mystery of him deepened. "My pleasure, Your Lordship." She rose to her feet. "Keep an eye on George and don't let him rampage about as per usual until that wound heals."

"I will." The earl scooped up his dog and then left the room without another word or a backward glance.

Chapter Four

What the hell is wrong with me?

Leaving so abruptly had been the height of rudeness. With a sigh, he glanced down at the dog in his arms. "Don't look at me like that." But the beagle continued to regard him with sad eyes as he stood in the corridor just beyond the parlor. "I realize my behavior was rude, and she did a good job with your leg." When the dog whined, he sighed again. "Yes, she was rather interesting in a plain sort of way." The thump of George's tail against his side said the dog agreed. "Fine. I'll apologize."

With dragging steps, Evan returned to the parlor, and when he entered and Miss Smythe looked up at him with confusion, heat climbed up the back of his neck.

"Lord Stanton. Is something amiss? Did George tear at his stitches already?" Concern wove through her voice.

"No. Nothing like that, so please, set your mind at ease." The fact she cared so much for an animal not her own had his respect rising. "I wish to apologize for my boorish behavior."

"It is quite all right, Your Lordship. You were under duress due to your dog's health."

"That is no excuse." After gently putting George on a nearby settee, he moved to a chair near to Miss Smythe's location. "I should have been more civilized and told you how grateful I am that you looked after my dog."

"And I probably should have kept quiet on your matrimonial prospects." She shrugged and sent him a wry glance. "It's a bit of a sore subject with me as well."

"Ah." Who was this bit of womanhood to tell him that he needed to do his duty?

She rose with a quiet elegance he admired. "Will you stay to tea, then?"

"Yes." Another wave of heat went up the back of his neck. "Thank you."

"You're welcome." As she passed the settee where George sat, she patted the dog's head. "Behave yourself. You have that gleam in your eye." The dog's tail thumped with enthusiasm. "I'll ring for a snack George can enjoy. I have found beagles especially like chicken liver mixed with chicken meat and peas."

"You have a beagle?" His eyebrows lifted with his surprise.

"She's not mine, really." Miss Smythe tugged on the green brocade bell pull, and for the first time he realized the parlor was decorated in varying shades of green shot with the faintest gold silk. Obviously, the squire had decent taste. "Bess wandered into my barn a few months ago. A few days back, she gave birth to a litter of puppies."

"Well, damn." Evan cast a glance to his own dog, who had a tendency to roam the countryside. "I apologize again if George is the father."

A blush stained her cheeks. "I wouldn't know if that is true, Your Lordship." Then she cleared her throat. "About the paternity, not your apology." When a footman came to the room, she ordered the food for the beagle and after, returned to her perch on the low sofa.

How... charming. When was the last time a lady blushed in his presence? Though past the first and perhaps second blooms of youth, she couldn't be much older than five and twenty. She was an interesting lady, not a beauty by any stretch, but there was an enchanting quality about her, a bewitchment, an understanding in her eyes. The slant of her dark eyebrows and the dark brown curls that escaped the messy knot at the back of her head practically beckoned him to come closer.

"Is your father at home?" He might as well discover other things about her since Chatham Cottage was the property closest to his.

A trace of sadness went through her moss-green eyes. "Unfortunately, Papa died some years back. My brother Thomas is the squire now, but he isn't at home. Either he's riding or attending to his duties as a magistrate. When he's in the country, that takes up much of his time."

"I see. Then that leaves you by yourself."

"Yes." She poured out another cup of tea and offered it to him. "I don't mind. That gives me the opportunity to do my rounds and check on the health of the various animals in my care."

When their fingers brushed, electric heat shot up his arm to the elbow. How strange. There was a nurturing air about her that tugged at him. Would she nurture people like she did animals? Could she find a way to fit together the broken pieces of himself as easily as she'd mended George's leg? Suddenly, he wanted to know. "How have I never met you before if you are the daughter of my neighbor?"

Miss Smythe shrugged. She kept her gaze on her own teacup. "You are probably in Town a good portion of the time."

The footman returned just then, and she directed him to put the bowl of chopped meats and veg onto the settee next to George. With a woof of either thanks or gladness, the damned beagle scrambled to his feet and tucked into the offering with gusto.

Evan couldn't help his chuckle. "I rather think you will be his best friend now."

"No one could take your place in that regard." When she met his gaze, she gave him a timid smile. "It is obvious he's well cared for."

"Indeed. Spoiled, more like it." Then he realized why he'd never met her before. "You don't like to socialize. It's why I've not seen you around."

"Not particularly. I'm the typical wallflower, I suppose. Dancing and talking to people makes me want to run and hide."

He snorted with humor. "Somehow, I rather doubt you are a typical *anything*."

"Oh." Another blush stained her cheeks, and it was as captivating as the first. "You would be sorely disappointed, then, Lord Stanton. I'm a country nobody whose brother wishes her to marry off with alacrity so he can resume his life." She paused to sip her tea, and he admired her slender fingers, the smooth skin of her elegant neck, the enticing curve of her breasts beneath the day dress of maroon. "I don't aspire to move within the *ton*, and I certainly don't wish to be *merely* someone's wife."

"I see." How very interesting. Didn't all women hunger after a title, position, and a family? "What do you aspire to be?"

"All I want to do is heal wounded and hurting animals." A dreamy expression crossed her face. "Ideally, I would like to open a clinic or a small office somewhere. Or barring that, I could travel throughout the county ministering to animals."

Impressive, and his admiration for her rose. After draining his cup, he said, "It is a lofty goal." And only made her more fascinating.

"Perhaps." When she looked at him, there was an agedness to her that appealed and spoke to his soul. "Do you ever think you were put on this earth for one specific purpose, and it is physically painful if you are not doing that?"

What was this? Never in his life had he met another person who seemed to understand what he felt. "Actually, I do."

"Oh?" Interest lit her eyes. "How so?"

Evan nodded. "For as long as I can remember, even when I was a boy, I have been fascinated by the stars. Studying them. Charting their movements. Finding the constellations. Watching comets. Locating other planets. Learning everything I could about the heavens." Excitement bled through into his voice. "Seeing what there is to see that is beyond my world here. Just me and my trusty telescope."

When she smiled this time, it had the force of a handful of suns. "Why haven't you devoted yourself to that? You obviously have a passion for it."

"I am an earl." As he shrugged, some of the enthusiasm faded. "I do these things when time permits, and especially when I'm here far from the lights and noise from London." For long moments, he peered at her while George finished up with his treat. "Out here, in the great expanses of rolling country, it's nearly magical… if I believed in that." A note of bitterness crept into his voice. "I cannot help but think there is so much importance to be found in those stars, so much we don't know about any of it."

"It seems to be a vast subject that will take many decades to understand."

"Oh, indubitably. Centuries, even." He nodded. "I dream about the moon sometimes, lay awake at night wondering what it must be like, to imagine if humans will ever advance enough to soar through those heavens or perhaps touch the moon."

For the space of a few heartbeats, they stared at each other before she broke the silence. "It all sounds so amazing, Your Lordship. I should like to see the stars for myself merely to discover why they fascinate you." Her grin nearly sent his world tilting. "If studying the heavens is something that makes you happy, by all means, pursue it. Life is too short to do one's duty all the time."

"As much as I would like to follow my heart, responsibilities to my title come first." The sadness pouring over him almost stole his breath. "I don't know if I'll ever have an opportunity to do that if I marry and have children. Which, according to my mother, is my *only* task this holiday season."

"Oh, please don't think that." She leaned over and touched her hand to his. Intense sensation streaked up his arm. "Don't give up hope. There is time enough for everything."

Why was there such a connection between them? "There is not much I can do in this life. It is what's expected of me."

Understanding filled her eyes. "If I intend to find a way to have my dream, you can too." Then she gave him a soft smile that had interest flowing to a completely different section of his anatomy, and he reeled from it. "That's a promise I can make as sure as snowflakes at Christmas."

"Ah." Though he didn't adhere to her notions of magic, Evan couldn't help but grin. "Why are you certain there will be snow in three days? The weather isn't conducive as of yet."

"Why not?" Miss Smythe shrugged. The faint scent of lilacs teased his nose. "It's as easy to be hopeful as not, Your Lordship."

Well, that was beginning to rankle. "Please call me Evan, or Stanton if you prefer." But he did not. He wanted to hear his Christian name on her lips. "You nursed my dog. We are beyond formalities."

"Oh, Evan is a lovely name!" She glanced shyly at him, and in that moment, he could see her as the wallflower she'd described. "I'm Christiana, but don't make use of that name around my brother. He'd have an apoplexy."

Good lord but the name seemed as if it had come from the heavens themselves. So melodious, beautiful even. "Perhaps he would at that." He shared a laugh with her. "I promise. Do you, uh, enjoy the snow?"

"To an extent. I have always thought it makes the whole world a bit lovelier. When everything is blanketed with white, sparling snow like a million diamonds—"

"—or stars?"

"Yes, just so." When she bestowed another smile upon him, he easily saw them twinkling in that gesture. "The world becomes a fairyland, where anything is possible, and…" The delicate tendons in her throat worked with a hard swallow. "Where I'm not quite as awkward in social situations, and where I might finally be understood."

"Ah. You refer to your brother's wish to see you wed." It wasn't a question.

She nodded. "I cannot help but feel this will prove the end of my dreams."

"Perhaps the man who might win your heart will manage to surprise you." As if he believed in love and romance. Who was he to give her advice on such matters? "But bear in mind such things are difficult, and love doesn't last."

"What happened in your life that has soured you from the wedded state?"

Well, hell. He was flying too close to the fire. "I would rather not share such a maudlin tale so early in our association." Not that he would see her again, for she and he didn't run in the same social circles.

"Does that mean you wish to foster a friendship?" That tiny bit of hope swimming in her eyes resonated with what he'd been feeling since she gave his dog stitches.

"Perhaps I do, and isn't that what this time of year is for?" The sugary sweetness of the words almost made him gag. Was it a lie, though?

"Somehow, I'm thinking you do not enjoy Christmastide as much as you don't believe in snow and magic."

"As I told my mother only yesterday, I will only believe in the magic of Christmastide if I see snowflakes fly by Christmas Eve." As he shrugged, Evan gave her what felt like a wry look. "Perhaps soon I shall reveal why."

Shock rolled through him from the admission. How exceedingly odd that it felt as if they were connected as if by an invisible thread. Not since Melissa had he shared anything like that with a woman. Should he explore it? Confusion plowed through his chest. He cleared his throat and set his empty teacup on the table. "Thank you for caring for my beagle. As you can see, he is quite in good spirits, especially after you've spoiled him with that food."

A low woof was George's answer, as well as an enthusiastic tail wag.

"He's a good boy." Christiana laid her cup on the table then she stood and relocated to the settee next to the dog. When she scratched behind the beagle's ears, the dog shivered and wagged his tail. He was quite shameful in his enjoyment. "No more playing near open windows. You do not have god-like powers," she told the canine and then hugged him when the dog climbed into her lap.

For the first time in his life, Evan wrestled with jealousy of his beagle. *What the devil is wrong with me?* Yesterday he was adamant he didn't wish to find himself matched with anyone, yet here he was, wondering if he might not change *her* mind on the same.

"Uh," he cleared his throat, for this was more difficult than he'd thought, "would you care to join me on a walk?"

"What?" Surprise jumped into her expression.

He rushed onward. "It's really quite lovely out there right now, and we can probably accomplish a good bit of exercise before it rains." Heat crept up the back of his neck. "I thought you might appreciate conversation not constrained to a parlor."

For long moments, she looked at the dog and he stared back. Then George barked and wagged his tail. Christiana smiled at Evan. "A change of venue is most welcome, but we shall leave George here." She peered into the dog's face. "Behave yourself while we're gone."

"Excellent!" Why the deuce was it suddenly so stifling in the room. The dog's whines followed them into the corridor, and Evan quickly closed the door to prevent him from escaping. "I suppose we could carry him with us in a basket."

"Absolutely not." She giggled as if that were the funniest joke. Since she was so petite in height, all he wanted to do was wrap her in his arms and tuck her head beneath his chin. "He can stay here and rest his leg, but I will show you the mother beagle in the barn, and her adorable puppies."

He couldn't think of a better way to pass the time. Perhaps it was best to ignore the maggot that had apparently gotten into his brain, for he somehow found the chit way too fascinating.

Chapter Five

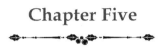

December 22, 1817
Stanton Hall

Christiana thought about Evan's words from the day before as she walked up the lane that led to Stanton Hall. Something had occurred in the poor man's life to leave him a touch bitter and not believing in the happiness of life. Because of that, she wished to help him regain that magic he lost. She might not move within the same level of society he did, but that didn't matter. If snowflakes for Christmas were the answer, she'd do it.

In fact, she'd already enlisted the aid of her maid and all available staff when they weren't preparing for their own Christmas festivities, for apparently, everyone knew of the earl and liked him well enough. Though he was young, he tried to follow in his father's footsteps, was kind to the people who worked his land as well as everyone else. They would stay up late cutting and fashioning a handful of paper snowflakes. If time permitted, they would make more.

Would he be surprised? That remained to be seen, but if it made him see things in a different light, the effort wasn't wasted.

By the time she reached the manor house, the swollen gray clouds of the overcast skies suggested rain might be imminent, which would make her walk back home uncomfortable, but she couldn't think about that now.

Ten minutes later, she was admitted into a lavishly appointed drawing room done in shades of blue. Not intending to stay long, she kept her ivory pelisse on as well as her bonnet. As soon as the elderly butler announced her name, Lord Stanton startled, and his paper rattled. George the dog raised his head from where he lay curled up on the Aubusson rug.

"Hullo, Evan, er, Lord Stanton," she quickly stammered. Heat sneaked into her cheeks. "I've come to check on my patient." Belatedly, Christiana realized she probably should have brought a maid with her, but she hadn't thought of such a thing, for she'd been alone for far too long to recall society's rules. Besides, she wouldn't be here long enough to hint at scandal.

The earl shot to his feet. "Uh, good morning, Miss Smythe." He tossed the newspaper aside. "As you can see, George is doing much better." With his chin, he gestured toward the dog. "Seems none the worse for wear."

"Good to hear." She kneeled on the floor and patted her thigh. "Come here, boy."

The dear beagle stood and came to her, only slightly hobbling. When he reached her location, he greeted her with an enthusiastic bark and a tail wag.

"Ah, look at you." As she held out a hand, the dog put a paw into her palm. "Such a clever boy." Before he could squirm away, Christiana took the dog into her lap. She gently removed the makeshift bandage. The wound was healing nicely. Then she replaced the bandage and patted his head. To the earl, she said, "Keep changing the dressing twice a day. I've brought some salve in my reticule."

"I appreciate your diligence." Evan propped his hands on his hips, which only brought her attention to his hips as well as his muscled thighs set off so splendidly in buff-colored breeches. "Do you ride, Miss Smythe — Christiana?"

Oh, how much did she adore hearing the sound of her name in his voice? But she frowned at him with a frown of confusion. The change in subject was a bit jarring. "I haven't ridden since I was a child. Now, there's no need for it. If I leave the property, I have a gig to take me into the village or I walk." Then she raked her gaze up and down his person. He was certainly dressed for riding, and she especially enjoyed the tweed waistcoat with the brown jacket. "I assume you do."

"Of course." When he offered a grin, flutters scudded through her lower belly, for the gesture transformed his face. "It's one of life's pleasures."

"I see." Though she didn't. "Where is your mother?"

"She's taken the carriage and gone visiting for the day, since many of her friends are back in Derbyshire for the holiday season." Then his expression brightened. "Come riding with me. I go every morning around this time in any event."

"Oh." Heat sank into her cheeks. "I'm not dressed for such an activity." To say nothing of the fact that she'd never been in a man's company who was so high on the instep.

"You are dressed well enough. Who will see?" He swept his gaze along her person, and she trembled. "It's overcast and no one will be about as it's too close to the holiday, which ensures that everyone is busy."

Where was the harm, really? And it had been ages since she'd ridden a horse. Cold apprehension twisted down her spine but threaded with excitement. Slowly, she nodded. "All right, but we leave George here. He is still healing."

As if the dog understood her words, he whined and returned to the spot on the floor near the fireplace where he'd been curled before.

"Agreed." Warm friendliness reflected in the earl's blue eyes. "Let us adjourn to the stables then."

After he retrieved outerwear, they arrived at the stables all too soon, Christiana was sorely tempted by the barn cats and a handsome pointer who greeted Evan with enthusiasm, but the earl had his mount brought around in short order. The black charger was gorgeous and had a white patch on his chest and another on the middle of his muzzle. Without delay, Evan swung himself into the saddle. Then he hefted her up with the help of one of the grooms. When she settled in front of him with her legs hanging over the side and a knee hooked over the pommel, his arms came around her.

Oh, dear.

"It is so high," she said in a semi-choked voice. As the horse danced impatiently beneath her, she clung to the earl's shoulders, but it was his arms around her sent confusion twisting with excitement down her spine. To say nothing of being glad for his warmth.

His chuckle tickled through her chest. "Will you be all right?" he asked as he manipulated the reins. The rumble of his voice in her ear was quite delicious.

"I think so." Oh, it had been such a long time since she'd ridden, and it was delightful to indulge again.

A companionable silence fell over them while they rode out. The scenery was beautiful, and even though it was overcast, everywhere she looked was glorious. Midway through, there were no tenant cottages or sheep. Being alone with this man left her in a constant state of heightened awareness. Did he feel it too? The invisible connection that had cropped up so quickly had taken her by surprise. It was heady enough, but she didn't know what to do about it.

As she glanced about to look at every view possible, she nearly lost her balance. A terrified squeak left her throat, but the earl was right there to catch her. He held her tight against his chest while tugging on the reins, which brought the horse to a stop, but his gaze bored into hers, and her breath stalled at the intensity in his eyes.

Before she could say anything, Evan lowered his head and gently claimed her lips with his. Flutters filled her lower belly, for this was her first kiss. She was caught off guard and inundated with the heat of embarrassment, but the pressure of his mouth against hers was lovely. As her eyes shuttered closed, she sighed and relaxed into his embrace, fully expecting to enjoy the wonder of that kiss.

Yet the earl pulled away. "Oh," she uttered as cold disappointment went down her spine. "For a first kiss, that was quite exciting." The whispered admission brought heat into her cheeks, but Evan chuckled, and she smiled.

"A first kiss from me?"

"My first kiss. Ever." What would he think of her? Surely this man so high on the instep had had lovers before, had kept women more sophisticated. Christiana laid a hand against his chest, couldn't stop staring at his sensual lips, wished to feel them on hers again. "I rather liked it."

"So did I." The man must have been of the same mind, for he kissed her again as if he had all the leisure time in the world and didn't mind investing that time into teaching her how to properly kiss.

It was magical. Her life would never be the same.

The sensation of falling assailed Evan. He'd forgotten how much he enjoyed kissing women, but then, he supposed the woman in question made the difference. And Christiana was that; he'd never met anyone quite like her. Would that they weren't on the back of a horse, for this position didn't allow for the most satisfying of embraces, but she was yielding and warm, and her lips so inviting with their petal softness that he drank from her the best he could. The fact she was inexperienced was a bit of an aphrodisiac.

I am the first man to introduce her to such things. It was a powerful responsibility indeed.

He moved his hand up to cup her cheek, but due to the awkward position and the slant of the edge of her bonnet, he couldn't gain the traction or the depth he wished. Still, she met his kiss with sweet curiosity and a trembling hand, and suddenly, he wanted to know much more about her.

Eventually, commonsense returned. Evan pulled away. "I beg your pardon. That wasn't well done of me." He'd taken a liberty he shouldn't have without at least asking her permission. When she stared up at him with round eyes full of surprise and bemusement, his shaft twitched. "I hadn't meant to; it merely happened." Because she'd looked so damned beautiful with her eyes full of delight merely from being on a horse.

"Isn't that the best kind of happenstance?" When the December breeze blew, she shivered. "I haven't taken offense. As I said, it was quite pleasant." When she touched a gloved fingertip to her lips, his chest tightened.

"Good." As the horse stamped with impatience, he grinned. "If you didn't mind that trespass, I suppose you won't mind this one."

Knowing she was cold, he opened his greatcoat and then bundled it about her, which meant he was obliged to hold her closer. Was it his imagination or did she utter a tiny sigh? "Do you wish to go back to the house?"

"Not really. It's rather lovely out here even if we're expecting rain instead of snow."

Why did the chit have her heart set on snow for Christmas? "I agree." His assessment had nothing to do with the weather or the countryside, and that surprised the hell out of him. For far too long he'd kept his heart aloof as a way to protect it. Had that been the wrong reaction after all? Not knowing, he set the horse into motion once more. "Do you have traditions you keep for Christmastide?"

"Not since my parents died." A tremble moved through her and transferred to him. Was she missing her parents or was his presence unsettling her? He sincerely hoped it was the latter. "Mama used to have great joy in Boxing Day activities, though. That was one of my first memories of her, since she died in childbirth."

"I'm sorry to hear that." Losing one's parents was devastating.

"Thank you." She burrowed closer to him, and he held his breath, for it felt all too wonderful. "It didn't matter we didn't have vast wealth. She would save up all year so she could prepare as many boxes as she could." Admiration wove through Christiana's voice.

"She used to knit mittens for the village children and mufflers for as many adults as she could manage. I adored her heart for service."

The more he heard about her and her family, the more he wished to know. "You function along the same lines with your talent for healing sick animals."

"I suppose." This time, her sigh was audible. "Since it's just me and my brother, Christmas has faded over the years. We have never had a big family, but now, we don't go through the trouble of decorating or collecting fir boughs or any of that, and some years, my brother stays in London without coming home here."

"And you're left alone." His heart squeezed, for he well knew exactly how that felt. Where she still retained a love for the holiday, he did not.

"Yes." When she nodded, the faint scent of lilacs became more prominent. It reminded him of the summertime at this very country estate. "I suppose that's another reason why my brother wishes for me to marry. To stem those feelings."

"I'm sorry." That sounded uncaring. "I mean, that you are on your own, not for possibly marrying. No doubt you will make someone a lovely wife, but I understand how lonely life can be." Damnation, but he was making a cake of himself.

"I don't know about that. In fact, my brother has demanded I attend your Christmas Eve ball so I might be inspected by eligible men." She huffed and fiddled with a button on his coat. "I am terrified to be out in society."

"Well, I shall be there, so you won't be alone." The muscles in his abdomen clenched each time her fingertips brushed over his waistcoat. What would it feel like to have her hands glide over his skin? Shoving the wicked thoughts away, he remained silent for long moments as he debated with himself over what to say next, for he certainly didn't wish to part company with her so soon. Finally, he heaved a sigh. "Feeling alone is part of the reason I have George."

"Oh? What's the other reason?"

A lump of emotion lodged in his throat. Where was the harm in telling her his history? "Ten years ago, I'd planned to give George as a puppy to my then-fiancée. However, she contracted an ailment of the lungs and died shortly before Christmas." To his mortification, tears sprang to his eyes, and he held Christiana a bit closer. "The beagle is all I have to remember her by. I still miss her."

"Of course you should. It's only natural."

He nodded. "I loved her. Gave her my heart," he forced out from a tight throat.

"Ah, and that is why you detest love and romance." She tipped her chin up and met his gaze. "I am sorry you were devastated. Death isn't easy regardless of who died. When you should have been planning a wedding, you had to let her go into death's arms."

"Yes." He blinked away the moisture from his eyes. "Now you know why I don't care for this time of the year."

"Isn't ten years a long time to mire yourself in maudlin feelings that blind you to the beauty going on all around you?"

Out of all the things she could have said, he didn't think that was it. "I am grieving." Why did no one understand that?

"There is no timeline on how long grief will last or how intense it will be, but letting that become a crutch on why you cannot move forward is just as debilitating."

"What do you know about it? You're still young." His hackles were up, and he didn't know how to calm.

She snorted. "Five and twenty is not exactly young. Regardless, my parents are both dead, Evan. Do you not think I've mourned for them?" It was the note of annoyance in her voice had a grin tugging at the corners of his mouth.

"Once more, I apologize. It seems I have been out of practice conversing like a gentleman."

"Because you have kept people away." Christiana patted his chest. For the space of a few heartbeats, she regarded him while his pulse increased. "Perhaps you might come to look at everything differently this year."

"Why?"

When she shrugged, her shoulder moved against his chest and tiny fires lit in his blood. "While there is no shame in grieving, nothing is gained by closing yourself off from life. I felt that way too once my father passed on. It's easier to hide in grief and not let anyone close for fear of losing them. Perhaps you should use the ball this year to put that theory into practice. You might find you enjoy courting."

What was this, then? Evan huffed in annoyance. "Are you trying to side with my mother in matching me?"

"No." Her tinkling laughter caught him unawares so much that he yearned to hear it again. "I am merely saying you should let yourself enjoy living again. You might find a new reason to smile."

He was coming terribly close to grinning like an idiot. In her company, everything suddenly felt… better. "I shall think about it."

"I'm glad." She nodded. Nothing except honesty shone in her eyes as she held his gaze again. "I don't like to think of you being unhappy."

"Why?" Confusion went through his chest. "We have only just met." Yet he'd kissed her, so what did that make him?

"I know, but it makes me sad to think you might be unhappy. Christmastide is such a joyful time of year, and since I look forward to it every year, I want you to do the same." Again, she shrugged then frowned. "I can't explain it more than that. It hurts me to know there is someone around me in pain."

Well, damn. Those red lips were not made for frowning. What could he do to bring back her smile? "Ah." Warmth filled his chest. It was rather lovely that someone besides his mother cared. Did that mean she felt the odd and immediate connection between them too? There was no way to know that, but every time her hip rubbed against his shaft as the horse walked along, interest of another sort slammed into him. "I appreciate your insight, Christiana." Truly, her compassion went beyond caring for the area's needy animals.

Then she *did* grin, and everything made sense in his world again. "Will we be friends after this? You are my neighbor, and this ride *has* been rather interesting." The dearest blush colored her cheeks.

"Of course." Yet the longer he had her in his arms, the more he talked to her, he didn't know if he wished to keep their relationship to a friendship, but was he ready for a romance? Was she correct in saying he couldn't continue to lose himself in grief? Or worse yet, was he using it as a shield to keep people away? There was much to think about. "Friends call on each other frequently, though."

"Indeed." Her smile encouraged him to do the same. "I'll need to drop by and peek in on George tomorrow regardless."

"Good." How long had it been since he'd looked forward to anything? "I've rather enjoyed our time together today." Was it possible the arrival of a young lady could pull him from the doldrums he'd been in for far too long?

Only time would tell.

Chapter Six

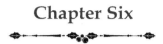

December 22, 1817

Christiana wrapped the folds of her cloak more tightly about her person as she trod along the lane that led to Stanton Hall. She'd already paid a call to check on the health of a farmer's sheep, a tenant's pregnant cat, and a random goat she saw hobbling along the side of a field.

Once she visited George the beagle at the manor house, she would go home and continue to work on making more paper snowflakes. Already, between her, the maids, and the footman, they had managed to fill two smallish boxes with the ornaments. Between now and the ball, they should have at least another one ready.

As they had a tendency to do, her thoughts returned to the earl and how lovely those stolen kisses with him had been, how everything seemed just a bit sharper and more colorful since that had happened. What a ninny she'd become, nurturing an inappropriate infatuation for a man so far removed from her station. Her brother would make jest of her, surely, if he ever found out, but she couldn't help it. Evan had been the only man to kiss her or even treat her as if she'd mattered, and that connection between them was puzzling.

"Miss Smythe! Fancy seeing you out and about today."

She glanced backward over her shoulder at the hail in *his* voice. Tingles of anticipation went down her spine. "Lord Stanton!" As she stood there on the lane, he urged his horse to her position, and she couldn't help but admire his powerful form astride that mount. "Out for a bit of exercise?"

"I am, and I wished to make use of the day before it rains. Though, from the way the temperature is dropping, it just might snow soon enough." When he grinned and his eyes twinkled with welcome, flutters went through her belly. "Where are you off to?"

"To pay a call on George to see how he fares."

"Excellent! If you don't mind riding again, I can take you since I'm returning home in any event."

Oh, dear. Riding with the earl? Was he remembering that kiss too? But there she was, nodding like a widgeon. "That would be lovely. Thank you." She patted the horse's muzzle. The equine blew out a breath of welcome in response.

He offered her a hand. "Put your foot on mine if you can. I'll pull you up the rest of the way." Once she did as instructed, he hefted her up as if she weighed nothing. "Here we are."

"Oh!" How amazing to be perched up so high. As soon as his arms went around her, Christiana shivered and arranged her skirting over her legs. There was naught to do but clutch his shoulder and settle in against him. His crisp, clean scent wafted around her, and she sighed with pure contentment as he put them into motion. For the next few minutes on the ride to the hall, she could pretend she wasn't a societal failure and that he might be more than a friendly neighbor to her. "Thank you for the ride."

"You are quite welcome. Seeing you has brightened my outlook for the day considerably." The low rumble of his voice so close to her ear sent a host of tingles down her spine. "You look a bit fatigued, Christiana. Is all well?" The warmth of his breath skated along her cheek.

"I, ah…" The heat of embarrassment slapped at her cheeks, for some of her sleeping time had been sacrificed for making dozens of paper snowflakes. "Please, do not worry. All is well with me. My rest is not as restorative as it could be." But once his ball had concluded, she would return to her previous patterns.

"Ah." As he manipulated the reins, he tucked her tighter into his arms, and she stifled a sigh. Would he try to kiss her again? "While riding this morning, I had a thought, and it was directly as a result of our conversation from yesterday."

"Oh?" Her heartbeat kicked up faster.

He nodded. "Would you have an interest in helping to gather fir boughs, ivy, and possibly mistletoe if we can find it? I really don't know what is available on my estate, for I've not explored with that in mind."

Excitement buzzed at the base of her spine. She glanced upward into his face. The rakish tilt of his top hat over his left eye did silly things to her heart. "Of course. Will we go now?"

"After you check on George. No doubt he'll be anxious to see you again." Pleasure wove through his voice. "Besides, it'll be an easier go if we bring out a carriage or a wagon to carry the greenery."

"It sounds like a lovely outing." Christiana tried to tamp her enthusiasm so he wouldn't think her desperate. "How has George been?"

"Better. It's difficult to restrain him now. He wants to be out doing things."

She chuckled. "I can imagine. No doubt he is a handful at full health."

"Oh, yes."

"How is your mother?"

"Well enough. She is mired in the last details for the ball. I'll probably see her at dinner."

All too soon, they arrived at Stanton Hall. After he'd guided the horse over to the mounting block in the stable yard, one of the grooms assisted her off the charger's back. Then the earl dismounted, and she stifled a sigh, for she missed his warmth and the unexpected security of being in his arms, albeit for a ride.

Once he'd escorted her inside to the parlor where the beagle was being kept in forced confinement so he couldn't tackle the stairs, Evan chuckled when George sprang to his feet and gave a bark of welcome. The dog's tail wagged so enthusiastically, she couldn't help but laugh while he bounded over as if his leg hadn't been hurt at all.

"Hallo, George." Immediately, she kneeled and giggled when the beagle proceeded to climb all over her in an effort to lick her face. "Obviously, you are feeling better." As best she could, Christiana examined him while the earl spoke with both the butler and a footman. "In my opinion, you are well on the way to healing and if you're careful, you'll suffer no ill effects."

The dog barked and licked her face, to which she giggled again.

"I appreciate your diligence with him." The earl watched her with a lazy grin and speculation in his brandy-hued eyes.

"You are most welcome." Then she frowned. "Why do you look at me like that?"

"It is nothing." He shook his head. "Ready to go on our errand? A few of the footmen are willing to come out with some tools for sawing. The butler suggested we find an evergreen tree to decorate before the ball like they do in the Bavarian region. It's not a popular request but does make for a cozy addition."

"That sounds intriguing." And would look so pretty with candles and ribbons. "And yes, I'm eager to start." She patted George's head. "Behave while we're gone.

The beagle howled as they left the room and closed the door behind them.

One thing about the earl was when he made plans, they were efficient. Twenty minutes later saw the greenery gathering party deep into a wooded area not far from the manor house. The wagon had rumbled along the ground and threw her more often than not into Evan's side, which made her laugh. Everyone else did too, and it was a rather merry time.

"All right, let's gather fir boughs that look robust, and one of you needs to scout out a nice, fat evergreen that we'll put in the drawing room. My mother would appreciate the effort. Also, holly branches will make delightful arrangements in vases." When Christiana met his gaze, her shrugged. "So says my mother." A flush rose above his collar. "My former fiancée was also partial to the plant."

"Then we shall need copious amounts of it," she agreed with a nod at one of the footmen. She gathered the folds of her cloak around her as a chilly wind blew over her person. "Perhaps it will snow soon."

The earl snorted. "As if that will usher in some hitherto unknown magic?" he asked in a soft voice as he took an axe in hand and followed the others deeper into the woods.

"One never knows." But she smiled. Christmastide had the power to change anyone if they were willing.

Gathering fir boughs was an enjoyable experience. Soon, the sharp scents of pine and wood filled the air, and tidy little piles of greenery were stored in the wagon's bed. However, locating ivy and mistletoe proved more difficult. Christiana left that task to the men, for she'd spied holly bushes growing in a nearby hedgerow.

A few snips of the scissors she was given soon had a bunch of the foliage overflowing the basket she carried. The dark green leaves and red berries looked pretty and inspired her to try her hand at making a couple of arrangements around tall candles for her own house. When a snatch of masculine laughter rang out, she glanced in the earl's direction. A sprig of the holly would look rather dashing pinned to

Evan's greatcoat lapel. Then she shook her head. Such a silly notion. She had no right to be thinking of him in any way whatsoever. Regardless of how she was beginning to feel about him, he was well beyond her reach.

Eventually, she wandered back to the group with her basket over her arm. Once more, the earl stared at her, this time his expression was inscrutable, but he looked as if he'd never seen her before. "I found some holly." Christiana smiled.

"So I can see." He smiled back. "It's quite beautiful, but something is missing." While the footmen gathered the cut greenery, the earl closed the distance between them. He broke off a sprig of the holly and gently tucked it behind one of her ears. "Now the picture is perfect."

"Oh!" She trembled when his gloved fingers barely brushed her cheek. Her lips parted when he leaned closer regardless of the fact they weren't alone. *Merciful heavens, is he going to kiss me again?*

"We found mistletoe, Lord Stanton!"

The shout from one of the footmen jerked them apart.

With an expression of regret, Evan turned toward the three men. "Excellent!"

"It's up in one of the oak trees, but someone will have to climb."

As he glanced at her once more, he winked. "I'll do it."

Alarm twisted down her spine. "You will injure yourself."

"Nonsense." He removed his top hat and handed it to her. "I shall be fine. As a youth, I often climbed trees." Then he moved to the oak the footman indicated. "Child's play, surely." He shrugged off his greatcoat and gave it to one of the waiting men. "Wish me luck, boys." Then he proceeded to climb the tree.

"Oh, dear," Christiana whispered as she stood at the base with the footmen. "This is foolish." Yet she couldn't help but admire the earl's form as he climbed. The breadth of his shoulders captivated her; his tight backside had heat seeping into her cheeks when she wondered how it would feel in her hands.

"Don't worry, miss. The earl's a good sort. All will be well," one of the footmen assured her. She recognized him as the one who'd brought her supplies when she'd first visited George.

But the whole of her attention was on the man in the tree. She gasped when his boot slipped. "Oh, no!" As worry knotted in her belly, she bit her lip while he layered himself on a sturdy branch but then teetered. The pounding of her heart and the tightness of her chest made it difficult to breathe. But he waved then set out to slash away at the vine-like plant with a knife he pulled from his boot. As it fell, a footman gathered it, but her eyes never strayed from the earl.

The dratted man climbed down soon enough with all the grace of a jungle cat, looking hale and hearty and none the worse for wear. Flutters moved through her lower belly, for he was just so handsome and muscled and virile.

And aggravating in the chances he took.

Once back on the ground, he took his greatcoat from the footman and regarded her with a wide grin. "See, Miss Smythe? Everything is fine, but I appreciate your concern."

"You could have fallen to your death!" Christiana wanted to rail at him for taking such a stupid chance.

"Yet I didn't." He winked at the footman, who snickered. Then he took his top hat from her and set it on his head at a rakish angle. "I was in full control the whole time, and it was well worth the effort to have mistletoe tacked in a strategic location of the ballroom. Lots of ladies to kiss on Christmas Eve, eh?"

"Oh... you!" Building into a temper with him, she shook her head and clutched her basket tighter. Why did she both want to smack him and kiss him? "Pardon me for worrying over your inconsiderate self."

"Oi! Christiana!"

She turned her head at the hail. A frown tugged the corners of her mouth downward as her brother rode up to their party. "Hullo,

Thomas." If there was no enthusiasm in her voice, she couldn't help it. The opportunity for a kiss from the earl had been lost.

"What are you doing out here, and without a maid?" Censure rode heavy in his voice while he handled the reins of his bay mare.

"Lord Stanton asked that I help gather greenery for his Christmas Eve ball, and since I was already at the manor paying a visit on his dog, I agreed."

"I see." Thomas cast a glance to the earl, who stared at her brother as if puzzled.

"I just didn't think to bring a maid on such an errand." Again. Heat went through her cheeks, for she'd wished to be in the earl's presence alone. "Thomas, this is the Earl of Stanton. Your Lordship, this is my brother, Thomas, the squire."

"A pleasure to meet you, Your Lordship," her brother murmured and extended an outstretched hand.

"Indeed." Evan clasped the hands, but that didn't stop the men from sizing each other up as the footmen put the last of the greenery into the wagon bed.

When they began chatting as if she didn't exist, cold disappointment spiraled down her spine. All the specialness of being in the earl's company faded, for he would no doubt forget about her now that Thomas had arrived.

"Well, I really should return home. I am somewhat fatigued," Christiana mumbled as she retreated into herself. Once more, she felt the unwanted wallflower and very much an intruder in a world that had no place for her. "Thank you for an entertaining morning, Your Lordship."

Immediately, the earl looked at her with concern in his expression. "At least let me offer you and Sir Smythe luncheon before you go."

Thomas drew himself up to his full height. "We shall gladly accept that invitation."

"Excellent!" Evan closed the distance between her and him. "Perhaps you should ride with your brother, and I'll meet you at the house." Gently, he tugged the basket from her lax fingers, and then in a lowered voice added, "Will you help decorate tomorrow? I would have no idea where to place all of this greenery. It is sadly not my forte and it needs to be done quickly. Mother is already busy enough."

With a furtive glance at Thomas, who watched her with speculation, she nodded despite her misgivings. "I should be delighted." It wasn't often she was able to enjoy such a lavishly decorated home like that of the earl's, and it would place her in Evan's company yet again.

"I look forward to tomorrow." Then, without another word, he put his hands on either side of her waist and more or less tossed her onto the saddle in front of Thomas. "Go gently, Sir Smythe. Your sister is a bit fragile. We wouldn't want her to catch a cold when Christmastide is her favorite time of the year."

"Not to worry, Your Lordship," Thomas replied as he settled his arms around her and flicked the reins. "If her health has gained your notice, I'll take more care than usual to see she's not worn out."

"I would appreciate that, for I owe your sister a debt. She nursed my dog when he fell into a spot of bother."

She stifled a sigh, but those darned butterflies took flight in her lower belly when Evan smiled, and the gesture crinkled the skin at the corners of his eyes.

Oh, Christiana, you ninny. You are falling in love with a man who is far beyond your reach. But that didn't stop her from beginning that slide. Perhaps it would serve as a distraction from the anxiety attending his ball would cause.

Chapter Seven

December 23, 1817
Stanton Hall

"I have it on good authority you have been spending time with the daughter of Squire Smythe recently."

Evan couldn't resist pointing his gaze at the ceiling. It didn't matter that he tried to read his copy of *The Times* or that he'd ignored his mother for the last half hour while they both occupied the drawing room, she still persisted in badgering him. "What of it? She's a charming young lady, and she attended to George after he fell out the upstairs window a few days ago." He shrugged as he folded his paper. "Now, she has consented to help decorate the manor house with Christmas finery, because I know how busy you are preparing for the ball."

One of his mother's eyebrows rose. "Since when have you thrown yourself into Christmastide with any sort of enthusiasm?" She laid her embroidery work aside to stare. "This is highly unlike you."

Heat crept up the back of his neck, but he ignored that. "Is not a man allowed to change his mind on a notion?"

"You can, of course, but it's suspect, since you've been adamant that we do not acknowledge the holiday for more years than I can count."

"Yes, well, I have my reasons." Evan focused his gaze on the newspaper print while George snored happily beside him on the sofa.

"Hmph." Her stare grew more intense. "Is one of those reasons a sudden interest in that woman? From what I understand, she has nothing to recommend her, and she certainly has no looks to speak of." When she frowned, he bristled and tossed his paper to the table at his elbow. "Or are you doing this to get back at me for suggesting you need to marry?"

"What are you saying, Mother? That Miss Smythe is not a good candidate?" Why had he said that? It wasn't as if he were contemplating marriage to Christiana. That notion hadn't even crossed his mind.

For the space of a few heartbeats, she regarded him with speculation. "My dear boy, don't think to throw your life or your title away on a woman of no social standing."

He snorted. "As if that matters."

"It matters to me. I want you to make an advantageous match, so your children can do the same. That is how it works in our world."

Dear God. Children. But the thought of having offspring with Christiana—to say nothing of the act that would lead to such—sent heat into his blood. "Do stop. As with the last time I promised to pledge myself to a woman, I will do so for love or not at all. Everything else cannot be contemplated, for life is difficult enough without having to wake up to a woman more concerned about wealth and position than the softer, more important things."

"You will get absolutely nowhere with that attitude." With a huff, she picked up her embroidery once more. "Marry for position, Stanton, then take a mistress for love. That is how the *ton* operates."

"Perhaps it is time for my generation to changes the rules." He scrambled to his feet. "There are happy *ton* marriages out there, and that doesn't mean marrying for love is something to sneer at." Despite the snit he was working up to, Evan crossed the carpet, leaned over his mother, and bussed her cheek. "Regardless, we will save this discussion for later. I have invited Miss Smythe here to assist in placing greenery and other Christmastide baubles because I know you are overworked as it is. Be polite to her. She is not accustomed to your sourness as I am."

"Where are you going?"

"My man of affairs is set to arrive soon, and I'll need to meet with him for a quick conversation, but I will join you here once that has concluded." Then he quickly left the room, for his thoughts chased around in his head like ponies on a loop, and they all had to do with a certain green-eyed woman for whom he was growing fonder of as the days passed.

An hour later, after his meeting had concluded, Evan made his way to the drawing room where the butler had informed him that Miss Smythe and his mother were decorating. They had already done the downstairs parlor as well as the entry hall. But once at the door, he held back, preferring to eavesdrop outside instead. It wasn't well done of him and not in the best of manners, but if he entered now, the conversation within would cease, and from all accounts, it sounded as if it could turn heated all too soon.

"Tell me about your people, Miss Smythe," his mother invited, and he recognized that saccharine tone. It was how she lured unsuspecting guests into her web. "I will admit I don't know much more about you than you are the daughter of our closest neighbor."

When Evan peeked around the doorframe it was to see his mother fussing with pine boughs on the mantel while Christiana artfully arranged boughs of holly and strands of ivy into a large bowl filled with clove-studded oranges and apples. The whole thing rested on a narrow table that ran the length of a high-backed sofa and would provide sweet perfume to the room.

"My father was the squire until his death a handful of years ago. He was quite a jovial man with the dearest laugh, but he rarely did that once my mother passed." Even at his distance, Evan heard the grief in her voice. "Sadly, she perished in childbirth when I was twelve."

"Ah, yes, I remember Evelyn Smythe. She was a Farthingham I believe before her marriage. One of the Viscount Willford's granddaughters." Was that surprise or pleasure in his mother's tones? Did she consider that pedigree good enough for him? Knowing her, probably not, yet it was a surprise to him.

"Mama didn't talk much about her life before she married." Christiana shrugged. "But I do know she wasn't keen to go back to London or move through society."

"A shame, for she was a beauty."

"I suppose I take after my father." A self-depreciating laugh escaped her. "In all my years living here in Derbyshire, we only went down to London a few times."

"For your Seasons, I would imagine," his mother prodded.

Evan peered into the room again. Red and silver glass balls were nestled into the greenery while Christiana placed a few tin bells into her arrangement.

"I had two, but they were both dismal failures." She paused in placing a red velvet bow amidst the fruit. "I'm afraid I am destined to be a wallflower instead of anything else, for I don't enjoy society all that much."

"What are your plans for your life? You must have some if you haven't yet snared a man."

In the corridor, Evan rolled his eyes. Why was his mother so waspish? Perhaps it was her way of protecting him from fortune hunters, but even a blind and deaf man would know that Christiana wasn't a gold digger.

"Thank you for asking, Lady Stanton. Since I vastly prefer to spend time with animals over humans, I would like to open a clinic or the like to care for and heal injured or sick animals. I'm quite partial to dogs, cats, goats, and sheep."

"Hmph." His mother sniffed, as if those aspirations weren't good enough. "There is not much room there to catch a husband."

Poor Christiana uttered a huff that signaled frustration. When Evan peeked into the room again, that was indeed the emotion lining her face. "I am not husband hunting."

"No?" His mother cackled with laughter, which she did just before she pounced. He had seen her destroy people higher in society than Christiana. "Then let me be truthful with you,

Miss Smythe. You have been underfoot a lot lately. Do you have designs on my son?"

From the corridor, Evan strained to hear her answer, and oddly enough, the breath stalled in his lungs, but he needn't have worried. She held her own while remaining polite against his mother.

"Lord Stanton and I are nothing more than friends, my lady. We only just met a few days ago, and anyone would be a fool to think any sort of romance could spring between two people in that amount of time." Her voice sounded farther away, and when Evan looked in again, she had finished with the arrangement and had moved to a table near the window where she fussed with a vase containing several fir boughs. "I simply wish for him to discover happiness in his life again, and if helping him enter into the joy of Christmastide does that, where is the harm?"

Evan stifled the urge to chuckle, but his respect for her grew. She had such a backbone, and the ability to think on her feet would serve Christiana well if he were to offer for her, ask her to be his countess. He held a hand to his chest as shock plowed through him. Was he truly there? As the drone of conversation continued, he tuned it out while pressing his back against the wall. Like she'd said, they had only known each other for a few days. Romance couldn't possibly spring between two people in such a short period of time.

Could it?

Yet there was that overwhelming connection between them that had prompted the kiss two days ago. Hell, when he'd seen her yesterday holding that basket of holly, when she had been irritated with him as he'd climbed the tree, when he'd put a sprig of holly behind her ear, he'd wanted to kiss her again merely to discover if that feeling from the first one had been a fluke or his imagination.

Did that amount to love or was his libido merely ramped too high from keeping himself aloof from women over the years?

He didn't know. It all required thought, especially since he'd fallen in love with his previous fiancée that fast as well.

"You are not exactly what society would consider proper or even pretty, Miss Smythe. I am afraid after the ball tomorrow I must ask that you don't come around any longer," his mother was saying, and the ice in her voice yanked him from his thoughts. "My son has certain responsibilities he needs to attend to above and beyond extending charity to an awkward neighbor who is firmly on the shelf."

Well, damn.

Before anything else was said that could create an ugly situation, Evan came into the room, pretending he didn't know they were there. "Oh. Hullo Miss Smythe. Have you been here long?"

"Long enough," she replied, and the vexation in her voice was all too evident. "However, I am just finishing. I don't believe any of the other rooms on this level need Christmas cheer."

Something akin to panic grew in his chest when he caught the look of victory on his mother's face. He couldn't lose Christiana merely because his parent refused to behave. "Would either of you care for tea? I find myself quite famished."

An expression of gratitude crossed the younger woman's face. "That would be lovely. Thank you."

"None for me, Stanton." His mother dusted her hands together. "I am going to check the progress of the ballroom decorations then I plan to lie down for a few hours before dinner. Recent... events have worn me out." With a speaking glance at him and completely ignoring Christiana, his mother left the room.

What the hell was that about? Not knowing, but figuring he wouldn't like it if he did, Evan yanked on the brocade bell pull while Christiana kept herself busy by starting on yet another arrangement in a vase. When a footman came to the door, he ordered tea with plenty of edibles then he crossed the room to her location.

"Can I take it from your scowl that my mother discomfited you?"

A blush stained her cheeks. "She doesn't like me very much. Fairly accused me of dangling after you." A shrug only lifted one shoulder, but it called his attention to her plum-colored dress and the innocent lining of lace around the bodice. "Of having designs on you."

Of course she was indignant, for she wasn't that sort of woman. "Please don't take anything my mother says to heart. If I had a duke's daughter working on these decorations, it still wouldn't be good enough for her."

Christiana snorted. "That's doubtful, but at least a duke's daughter has a pedigree that would pass muster with Lady Stanton."

"My mother's opinions have no bearing on who I wish to have in my life." Unable to be parted from her, Evan closed the distance between them. "I invited *you* because *I* want you here, not to see if you would pass an inspection." Gently tugging a fir branch from her fingers, the pungent scent of pine wafted to his nose. "Understand?"

"I believe so." She nodded. "Thank you." Her chin wobbled. "While I enjoy being in your company and it's marvelously easy without me needing to feel less than anyone else, your mother makes me feel as if I'm naught but a country bumpkin who couldn't aspire to even be an upstairs maid in her household."

Before he could answer, the footman brought in a tea service on a silver tray.

"Just set it on the table there. Thank you."

"Of course, Your Lordship." The footman left without further conversation, but suddenly Evan wasn't in the mood for tea.

When he turned his attention back to Christiana, the light sheen of tears in her eyes completely gutted him. Protection for her welled in his chest. "Please know my mother doesn't speak for me." Daring much, he cupped her cheek as she trembled. "The connection between you and I is strong despite the fact we have only just met. Don't you think that should be explored?"

"I... I don't...." Confusion clouded her mossy green eyes, and when her gaze dropped briefly to his mouth, Evan was lost.

"Come here," he whispered. He slid his hand about her nape and dragged her to him then crushed his lips to hers.

As if a lit match were dropped onto dry straw, heated passion fairly consumed him as he moved his mouth over hers. When she slipped her hands up his chest to lock about his neck, her body naturally fit against his, all softly rounded curves that fit into his angles. With a groan, Evan deepened the kiss, swept the tip of his tongue along the seam of her lips, and as she tentatively opened for him, he tangled his tongue with hers, fencing with her until she parried in response.

The tiny moan and sigh of surrender she uttered strained his control, but he continued to kiss her as if his life depended on making her senses spin. Breaking the kiss, he dragged his lips beneath the underside of her jaw and as she shivered, he grinned. That skin was as soft as satin, and her fingers in his hair at his nape urged him onward.

"Evan... Oh!" She melted into him as he kissed a path along the side of her neck to follow the lace edging of her bodice.

"Mmm?" It was pure insanity how much he wanted this woman, for perhaps more than just a quick tryst in his drawing room. He walked her backward until the table by the sofa prevented further movement. How easy it would be to set her atop that table, put in her a state of dishabille so he could sample her charms. Would she let him?

Unfortunately, he wouldn't find out for loud barking from the corridor beyond warned him that George would be upon them imminently. With a groan, this time of regret, he pulled away and took two steps from her to put much needed distance between them.

"I believe your patient is coming to see you," he said but wished they were anywhere else with the privacy he wanted.

Christiana giggled, and the sound went straight to his stones and heightened his awareness of her. "He seems to always know when I'm in residence."

"Merely wishes to be everywhere you are," Evan said softly as he made his way around the sofa. Damn, but he wanted that too. "Perhaps we should have tea. Only then will I consent to let you return home. I'll even escort you there if you wish."

But it was growing more and more difficult to not be with her.

Chapter Eight

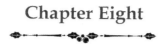

December 23, 1817

Christiana yawned. A glance at the carriage-style clock on the parlor mantel indicated the hour was nearly midnight.

"We need to pack all of this so we can arrive at Stanton Hall quickly," she told the two maids who were helping tonight with paper snowflakes.

The cut-out decorations were seemingly everywhere in the room she had designated for the crafting projects. Since her butler had spoken with the butler at Stanton Hall, they were assured of privacy and secrecy tonight when they would sneak the handiwork into the manor house. The footmen and maids there were ready to help hang and place the decorations in the ballroom so the earl would be surprised on the morrow.

A blonde-haired maid named Molly nodded. "One of the grooms is bringing the pony cart around, miss. We'll be there in good time." She would be the only one to make the trip tonight.

"Thank you." Christiana met the gazes of the staff that were in the room. "You have all helped tremendously and have gone beyond your duties. I appreciate that so much." But would Evan? That remained to be seen.

Another of the maids—Sarah—smiled. "You must care for Lord Stanton, miss, if you went to all this trouble." When Christiana's face heated, the girl continued. "I hope Sir Smythe doesn't have an apoplexy from your initiative."

"You and me both." Though knots of worry went through her belly, she didn't let it dampen her rising excitement. "Everyone deserves to know the joy of Christmastide, and since Lord Stanton has had a bit of a rough go during the holidays these years past, perhaps this gesture will pull him from his doldrums."

Molly giggled as she handed a footman one of the boxes brimming with snowflakes. "He might be so appreciative that he'll offer for you." She glanced at Sarah, and they both giggled. "It would be so romantic to see you as a countess, miss, and living in such a grand house as Stanton Hall!"

Oh, dear.

"I don't know about that, but this is the neighborly thing to do." The heat in her cheeks refused to fade as she took another box in her arms. "Come, Molly. Time is of the essence. The household will be abed, and if our luck holds, Lord Stanton will be out. We can decorate in peace." For she did so wish that Evan would see her handiwork shortly before the ball.

"Yes, miss." Molly picked up the last box and with a wink at Sarah, she followed along behind Christiana.

The darkness of the night was thick and complete as she and Molly wound their way silently up the lane leading to Stanton Hall. The air was markedly colder than it had been earlier in the week. Perhaps it would portend snow. Within that velvety background, millions of stars twinkled. If she asked, would Evan teach her about those very same stars? Could he show her the difference between planets and stars? It was something she needed to ask if she could get up the courage, for after the Christmas Eve ball, she would have no more reason to be in his company.

A glum mood remained with her while she eventually drew the pony cart up the circular drive, but instead of going to the front door, she guided the horse around to the kitchens, where the door was open and the butler as well as a few other staff members were waiting.

No sooner had the cart come to a halt than everyone jumped into a flurry of activity. Christiana and Molly were taken straightaway to the ballroom. Already, footmen and maids were on ladders and chairs, affixing the last trimmings to the fir boughs and branches already in place. Soft exclamations went up when they were given the boxes of snowflakes. Immediately questions began to fly, and everyone was suitably impressed at the craftsmanship and time involved in the making of such.

The warmth of their praise filled Christiana's chest, and she wore a smile the entire time she assisted the footmen and maids. Some of the snowflakes were hung from the ceiling; some were stuck to the walls and windows. After a few hours, she stood back to survey the final look.

"Oh, it's lovely!" It was as if the spirit of Christmas blew through the room and frosted the space with ice and snow. In addition to the hundreds of cut paper snowflakes, the footmen had glued sparkling white and silver glitter to some. They'd tacked silver foiled streamers to the walls and ceiling. "You have all done an amazing job." Tears misted her eyes. "The earl will be so surprised."

Please, Evan, believe in magic as well as romance again.

The possibility of anything occurring between them was almost laughable, for at the end of the day, she was so far below his station he would never take a chance on a romance with her. And that was all right, but she at least hoped by knowing him for a handful of days, she'd leave him with an adjusted mindset so that when he did choose a woman to be his countess, he would once more open his heart to the possibilities of love.

"It does look ever so different in here," Molly said with a fair amount of awe in her voice. "What you have done, miss, is outstanding."

Christiana's cheeks heated. "I don't know about that. I merely wished to bring a touch of Christmas to the earl's life."

Some of the footmen chuckled as the butler gazed about the room and nodded.

"You have done well, Miss Smythe. But perhaps you should go home now and take a well-deserved rest. It is nearly three in the morning."

"Dear heavens! I didn't realize it was so late." No wonder she was having difficulties keeping her yawning at bay. She squeezed Molly's hand. "Grab your outer things and wait for me at the stables. I'll be there in a twinkling."

"Of course, miss."

As Christiana stood in the middle of the ballroom admiring the transformation, she sighed. Yes, Christmastide was her favorite time of the year. It made her remember what she'd liked best about her mother as well as all the little hopes and dreams she still held for herself. Whether or not they would ever come to fruition didn't matter. For the moment, they were there in her heart, those tiny seeds planted, and she maintained if one believed hard enough, especially at this time of the year, that miracles could happen.

By the time she shook herself from her thoughts, the ballroom had cleared of servants. With a sigh, after gathering her cloak from where it had fallen on the floor, she donned it and made her way silently into the darkened corridor.

She sucked in a breath as a shadowy figure approached from the opposite direction. The race of her heartbeat prompted a stumble in her steps, but the closer the figure came, she recognized the height and build. Then his scent wafted to her nose, and she breathed a sigh of relief. "Lord Stanton." Surprise infused those two words. Obviously, he'd either been at the pub in the village or visiting some of the other neighboring gentry, for he was dressed in evening clothes but not nice enough to denote a big event.

"Miss Smythe." There was no mistaking the pleasure in his tones. "Why are you here?"

Oh, dear. She couldn't very well tell him the truth without ruining the surprise she'd worked so hard on in the ballroom. "I, uh…" *Think, Christiana!* However, dissembling had never been her strong suit. "I was worried about your dog, so I came over to check on him. I wanted to be sure he wasn't biting at his stitches."

"Did you have reason to suspect he was?" At the obvious worry in his voice, she frowned and moved to rest her hand fleetingly on his arm.

"There is always the chance, especially with a dog so exuberant as George, but he's fine," she rushed to assure him. Oh, she wanted so much to touch him, to rifle her fingers through his hair that had been displaced by the breeze, for he'd already shed his top hat and greatcoat, no doubt in the entry hall when he'd come in.

"Good." He nodded but stepped closer to her. The heat of him twined about her, teasing, calling… "Regardless, you shouldn't be here." His voice was a whisper, but his eyes glittered in the dim light. "It isn't proper."

"I know." It would be all too easy for him to take advantage of her with no one around and the night already fallen, but she didn't wish for the consequences of such a tryst, especially when there wasn't much hope of a future between them. But none of those thoughts prevented her from wondering about what he might look like without clothes, or what his hands on her body would feel like. With a poorly stifled sigh, Christiana shook her head. "I am on my way out, but it was lovely to see you again."

"It was." He lingered, made no move to let her pass, but then neither did she try. "Shall I escort you home?"

"That won't be necessary. I drove the pony cart and my maid is waiting in the stables. It's a quick trip, besides."

She felt rather than saw his frown. "But it's dark."

What a dear man he was. "It was dark on the trip over, Your Lordship." Even though her words were whispered, they sounded all too loud in the hush that had fallen over the house.

By increments, he closed the short distance between them. "It's not safe."

A tremble moved down her spine. "I shall be fine."

"If you are certain." Before she could answer, he cupped her cheek with a large hand, but when she assumed he would kiss her, he pressed his lips to her forehead. The tender gesture brought tears to her eyes. "All right." Too soon, he pulled away, and once more there was space between them. "I suppose I'll see you tomorrow at the ball."

"Yes, of course." Why did she wish to dissolve into a watering pot in this moment?

"You will save me a dance?"

Christiana snorted. "I am quite certain my dance card will remain free. No one wishes to engage a wallflower in conversation or anything else."

"I rather doubt that."

"We shall see tomorrow… or rather later tonight." A rush of intense sadness fell over her. "Good night, Lord Stanton."

"Good night, Miss Smythe. I wish you pleasant dreams."

As quickly as her feet would carry her, she fled along the corridor and through the bowels of the house until she breathed in the cold, outside air and gained the stables. Thank goodness the horse had already been harnessed to the cart, for she wouldn't put it past the earl to have gone back on his word and drive her home.

Molly eyed her with speculation as Christiana put the cart into motion. "Is all well with you, miss? You seem a bit flustered."

"It is nothing. Merely tiredness from sacrificing some of my sleep time to make snowflakes for an earl."

Once they gained the lane that would eventually connect to the road, she glanced backward, and her breath stalled. Evan was there astride his charger, as if they were pieces of the darkness. He kept a respectful distance with his horse barely moving as he followed them. The lovely man would escort her home even though she'd told him there was nothing to fear.

"Oh, dear," she whispered to herself and didn't care if her maid heard. Her heart fluttered like mad. Warmth filled her entire being. The earl would protect her when there was no need.

"I fear he might be a bit of trouble." The man was slowly worming his way beneath her skin, but she was a ninny to think anything could come of it. He was an earl; she was a nobody and had nothing to recommend her. Yet, here she was, falling for him a little bit more each day that went by. "What am I to do now?"

From her side, Molly snorted. "Let him pay his addresses, of course," she said in a soft voice. "You are obviously going tip over tail for him."

"Am I?" Of course, she didn't need to ask, neither did she need confirmation. It was something she felt deep down in her soul, but how much would it hurt after the ball when they went their separate ways?

"You are not that stupid, miss." Molly touched her gloved hand. "You care for him. That is nothing to sneeze at, and if he knows what's best, he'll return that regard."

"I'll wager it's a bit more complicated." Wasn't it?

The maid huffed. "For all your talk of magic and hope, why can you not believe it for yourself?" She nudged Christiana's hand again. "It is Christmastide, miss. If you have never believed in miracles before, at least do so tonight."

"I will endeavor to try."

When all was said and done, she still didn't want to go to the ball, no matter that Evan would be there, for then he would see just how unremarkable she was when she sat on the sidelines amidst the glitter and glamour, as well as all the elevated ladies of his world.

Chapter Nine

December 24, 1817
Christmas Eve ball
Stanton Hall

With an hour until his annual Christmas Eve ball, a feeling of restlessness assailed Evan. While he didn't want the hassle of doing the pretty with the area's movers and shakers, and he certainly didn't wish for matchmaking mamas — his own included — to shove every eligible woman at him during the evening, he couldn't back out now.

The hosting duties were expected of him, and people far and wide looked forward to this event all year. For all her flaws and annoyances, his mother had put great effort into making sure the ball would go smoothly, as well as the light supper that would follow for the people who wouldn't be going to midnight church services. It was to be held in the dining room buffet-style so the staff could enjoy their own festivities and go to church if they wished as well.

He'd been adamant about that.

And through the day, his thoughts had remained on Christiana. When he'd accidentally discovered her in the corridor last night, he'd known a powerful urge to abscond with her upstairs and take her to bed, but he'd exhibited restraint, for he hadn't wished to spook her, but having her close in the shadows had been all too intimate. He hadn't kissed her last night— couldn't—for his control would have snapped.

Which had made his thoughts run rampant and rob him of sleep.

Could he?

Should he?

Was there enough there?

He didn't know, and that prompted even more feelings of disquiet. There was one thing more he wanted to do before dressing for the ball, so he made his way to the ballroom. As of yet, guests hadn't begun to arrive, so the room was still very much empty, but as soon as he stepped foot into the space, his chest tightened as he marveled over the transformation.

"What kind of sorcery is this, then?"

Everywhere he looked, paper snowflakes, dozens and dozens of them, and all different styles, were tacked to the walls or hung from the ceiling as if a great winter god had scattered them upon the wind and now, they were trapped in his ballroom. Glitter, beads, and tiny spangles caught the candlelight and reflected it back so that the decorations sparkled like mad, as if they were truly snow in the moonlight. In each direction he turned, fir boughs, baubles, and red velvet ribbons were strewn about adding to the festive atmosphere. As he moved into the center of the room where the dancing would take place, he stared in open-mouthed astonishment.

An elegantly decorated evergreen tree — the one the footmen had cut a couple of days ago — stood twinkling in a corner with strings of smaller snowflakes. The glimmer and glitter all around fairly screamed out Christmastide, but over and over his gaze was pulled to the snowflakes. Evan pressed a hand to his heart as that organ squeezed, for the hours it must have taken to create all of those decidedly different paper ornaments astonished him and humbled him.

Who had set this miracle into motion?

Then he froze and the breath stalled in his lungs, for it was indeed a miracle where he'd not believed in them for a very long time. And what was more, he knew exactly who was responsible for them — Christiana.

"Well, damn." The softly spoken oath sounded overly loud in the hush. Perhaps the ball wouldn't be as horrid as he'd once thought. There was a certain happiness, a comfort in the sight of those snowflakes. "She made it snow. For me."

The feeling of falling down, down, down assailed him.

"Good evening, Lord Stanton."

The sound of her voice wrenched him from his thoughts. As she joined him in the ballroom, he couldn't help but stare. "Miss Smythe — Christiana — what are you doing here?" And damn if she wasn't the very vision of Christmastide. Her gown of dark green put him in mind of evergreens. Silver stitching on the brocade skirt was reminiscent of snowflakes while the bodice was of dark green velvet with short sleeves. Silver lace lined the top of the off the shoulder gown, and a silver satin sash drew his attention to the nip of her waist. The tails of it fluttered as she moved.

"What do you think? Will I blend in with your guests tonight?" When she executed a bit of a spin, he fell ever harder.

Silver lacing decorated the back of the gown. A choker on a silver satin ribbon circled her slender neck. A plain silver broach was pinned to the center and winked in the candlelight.

"God, yes." He couldn't say anything else, for the words were stuck in his suddenly tight throat. "You are enchanting." And with her brown hair piled high on her head and held in place with plain silver combs, it was all he could do not to sweep her into his arms and ravage the hell out of her.

Her smile rivaled the hundreds of candles in the room. "That is a lovely reaction. It is not a gown in the latest style, but with the alterations, no one will know." She met his gaze and he wished to dive deep into the cool pools of her green eyes. "I thought I would find you here."

"Why?" His voice was little more than a croak as he continued to stare.

"Because as much as I dislike crowds and being in society, you do as well, so it was only natural to assume you would wish to see your ballroom before it filled with guests."

How was it that she knew him so well? "Did you do this?" Evan gestured to the snowflakes and the enchantment therein.

"I did."

"When?" Truly, it was baffling.

Christiana shrugged. "Nights after I retired to my room. Early mornings before breakfast. I enlisted the help of my maid as well as a few others when they were off duty. Last night, your staff put the snowflakes up, which was truly why I was here." A giggle escaped her, and it was the most amazing sound he would always keep in his heart. "If I see another pair of scissors again, it will be too soon. I'm going to have calluses."

Bloody hell. The woman was incredible. "Why would you do this?"

"Why not?" When she smiled again, he continued that damned fall. "To help you believe in the magic of Christmastide, and perhaps in this way, you will find romance as well."

He forced a swallow into his dry throat, for he was no longer bitter about any of that. Because of her. "You assume I will dance with a woman tonight and the whole of my life will change?"

"It is not outside the realm of possibility." As her smile widened, he was all too glad he was lost.

"No, it is not." Perhaps it had already happened, and he'd spent the better part of the week denying it. This winsome wallflower, this woman whose heart was so large it had the capacity to love every living, hurting creature, and managed to thaw — heal *his* heart — and suddenly, he didn't want that feeling to end. To him, she *felt* like Christmas, that warmth and goodwill, that joy and lightheartedness… that magic! What he'd found in his previous fiancée, he'd discovered again with Christiana. It was all he'd searched for over the years but had never quite managed to track down.

And it changed everything.

"Well?" One of her dark eyebrows arched in question.

Damn, he'd lost the gist of the conversation. "Well, what?"

"Has my handiwork done the trick?"

Such a complicated question! "I... I am not quite certain."

"Hmm." She glanced about with a faint smile while a dreamy look appeared in her eyes. "Perhaps we should wait for the ball before you decide."

"I..." Suddenly, he couldn't chance it. To say nothing of the need to touch her. "Do me the honor of dancing a set with me?" He held out a hand to her and waited with bated breath for her answer.

An expression of surprise crossed her lovely face. How could anyone ever think her plain? That goodness of spirit shined through and made him wish—hope—he could follow in her stead. "Now?"

"Yes. Why not?" Evan wiggled his fingers. Though she was completely rigged out in holiday finery, he hadn't yet dressed in his formal attire. All the more reason to look forward to seeing her reaction later. "Please? No doubt much of my time will be spoken for once the ball opens."

"I suppose that's true." She slipped her hand into his. "This is probably the only time I will indulge in dancing tonight." A flash of sadness shadowed her eyes. "But this will be so much better without a crush of people."

"That is too bad, for you are an absolute delight." He took her into his arms. She felt all too right there. "And I wouldn't be allowed to hold you like this once there are tabbies and tattling tongues in attendance."

"Oh?" The look in her eyes gave him an odd uplift of hope. "I have found over the years that being alone isn't as dull as one might think. Within reason."

"Perhaps." Evan set them into motion while humming a few bars of a popular waltz. "Unless one has been alone by choice for far too many years and suddenly wishes for companionship, for... more."

Was that true?

"There is that," she said in a rather breathless voice.

Oh, he wouldn't be an earl if he didn't use the situation to his advantage, so he made certain to lead her into a continental waltz while he hummed a few strains here and there. After the first circuit through the room, he drifted to a halt with her still snug in his embrace, and as he peered into her eyes, he just *knew*. Again and again, he went tip over tail. This seemingly shy wallflower was who he wanted by his side for the remainder of his days; who he'd waited for this entire time while he'd kept his heart aloof from hurting. It didn't matter that his mother didn't approve, or that Christiana wasn't equal to his station, or that she never put herself into society. Nor did it matter that a romance after a few days was next to impossible.

He merely wanted *her*.

With a grin, he peered into her face. "Will you promise me a dance later this evening?" Oddly enough, he wished to show the area's elite that he was officially off the market.

"Oh, I…" Panic jumped into her face. "I am not sure about that. You will have much better ladies on your arm tonight."

"None of them will be you." He caught her head between his palms and kissed her. How could he not? The two they'd already shared were simply not enough and now he wanted more than that. In fact, he wanted a promise.

With each new meeting of their lips, with every touch of their tongues, the kiss grew more heated with so much in the offing that he didn't say. As she uttered a tiny moan, Christiana held onto his lapels, but she matched him kiss for kiss, and there was a sweet hunger there that fed his own. Evan dared to cup her breasts, dared even more to worry her nipples through the fabric of her gown. When those tips hardened and she gasped at the liberty, he fell even more. Damn, but they weren't truly alone so he couldn't coax that gorgeous gown from her shoulders and show her the depths of his regard.

"Evan…" Eventually, she put a hand to his chest and gave him a bit of a shove. "We shouldn't continue this. Not so close to the start of your ball. Guests will arrive soon." The breathless quality of her words endeared her to him even more.

"Are you frightened, sweeting?" Though he hadn't meant for the endearment to slip out, there it was. Shock ricocheted through him and the same was reflected in her eyes.

"I…" The delicate tendons of her throat worked with a hard swallow. A blush stained her cheeks. "A little. Yes."

"So am I." It was only natural to grin, for it was easy with this woman. The last time he'd had the courage to follow through on this level, it had ended poorly. What if fate took a new romance away again? *I cannot worry about that now else I'll lose her.* Evan cupped her cheek then the back of her head, reeling her into his embrace once more. "Ah Christiana." As if he couldn't bear being parted from her, he kissed her, drank from her, wanted to tell her without words how he was beginning to feel.

She looped her arms about his shoulders and fairly melted into him. Temporarily going insane, letting himself be inebriated on her, Evan walked her backward over the floor until a wall at her back prevented further movement.

"Evan…"

"Hmm?" It wasn't well done of him, but he needed to touch her skin. Slowly, ever so slowly, he drew up her skirting, slipped a hand along the heated, silky skin of her thigh to squeeze an arse cheek. When she squealed with surprise and need darkened her eyes, he sighed, brushed his lips along hers, and then released her before he embarrassed them both. His breath was slightly ragged from desire. "Promise me a dance later, Christiana. I cannot make it through to the end without you."

Her eyes widened but she nodded. "Very well. I have to…" Not finishing the thought, she turned about so abruptly her skirting flared around her ankles. Then she fled with that same skirt hiked in her hands.

"Well, damn." Truly, they were magic together, and he smiled. She was stronger than she assumed if only she would believe it, and certainly she was countess material. But was he truly contemplating proposing marriage?

Only time would tell, but first, he needed to confer quickly with his mother, adamantly tell her his choice had been made, search through the Stanton jewels for something appropriate to grace Christiana's slim finger, and then get himself ready for the ball.

All because of an influx of sparkling, paper snowflakes an area healer had made for him.

Chapter Ten

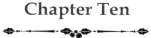

December 24, 1817
Christmas Eve ball

As a longcase clock in the corridor beyond the Stanton ballroom struck the midnight hour, Christiana watched from the sidelines as the party began to wind down. She was quite comfortable within the grouping of chairs with gilt-painted legs that had been set aside for fatigued companions or mamas as well as traditional wallflowers.

Though she'd given her promised dance to Evan early on in the evening, she'd been entertained by observing, and though she felt a certain affinity for her fellow unwanted wallflowers, she also wondered if any of them had been kissed as she had before the ball had begun, or if anyone of them had the dream of catching the eye of a handsome earl like she had.

If only for a moment.

It was impossible, of course, for nothing could come of that heated, soul-deep connection, but it was glorious to think about, nonetheless.

Then the earl was there before her, with his hand held out, asking her for another dance.

Christiana gasped. As did the girls sitting nearby. Multiple pairs of eyes were on her. A second dance with the same woman was tantamount to a proposal! And, oh, he was so handsome in his black evening clothes with his starched cravat done into a complicated knot. A silver satin waistcoat embroidered with white swirls reminded her of snow but teased his flat abdomen beneath. "I... I... Are you quite certain, Your Lordship?" she barely managed to force out from her suddenly tight throat.

"Oh, yes. *Quite*." He lifted a blond eyebrow while wicked intent sparkled in those rich brown eyes.

"All right." Her hand shook as she slipped her fingers into his palm and then he pulled her effortlessly to her feet. "Please don't listen to the gossip tongues once they try to tear your reputation — and mine — to ribbons."

A chuckle left his throat. The rumbling sound sent tingles spiraling down her spine. "I never pay them any mind."

The next set was a Viennese waltz. It wasn't as intimate or soul binding as the one she'd shared with him earlier in the empty ballroom, but it was the height of romantic by barely touching hands and elaborately circling partners, and she always caught her breath until the steps returned her to his side.

At the top of the room, he offered a tight smile then led her off the floor. When she offered a protest, Evan pulled her through the open double doors. Without a word, he took her hand and tugged her through the corridors. Once at the library, he quickly encouraged her into the room and closed the door behind them.

"Evan, what are you about?" Oh, but she suspected. Of course she did. She recognized that look in his eye, had seen it on too many of her friends' faces, had even spied it between dogs, cats, and other animals. Butterflies took flight in her lower belly.

"Tonight has shown me something I've unconsciously been searching for over the years. When I saw all the work and effort you put into with the snowflakes in the ballroom…" Emotion graveled his voice. An unexpected sheen of moisture sprang into his eyes, gone as he blinked it away. "Since I met you, Christiana, you have shown me time and again how caring your heart is, how you think of others, how you draw us all to you and make things better."

"What?" Excitement warred with foreboding in her belly as she stared at him. Surely, he wasn't leading up to what she thought he was.

From the pocket of his waistcoat, Evan pulled a ring. The gold band gleamed in the light of the few candles lit in the room, but the glitter from two small pear-shaped diamonds was dazzling. "Will you marry me, make me the happiest of men?"

She darted her glance from the ring to his face. Nothing except honesty and earnestness reflected in his eyes, yet she remained awestruck. An earl was offering for her! "How can this be happening?" Confusion sounded in her voice. "Surely you don't want a wallflower."

The deep rumble of his chuckle tickled through her chest. "That matters not to me. I want you, and I have from practically the first moment we met."

Good heavens. One of her hands crept to her throat and her fingers trembled. "You hardly know me."

The grin he flashed left her weak kneed. "I know enough. I know you've utterly captivated me. I know you've swept me up in your tide of hope and optimism and caring." He caught one of her hands in his free one. "I know I want more of that for the rest of my life."

Oh, dear! While her heart trembled, her brain refused to fall for the utter romance of the moment. "All of this is too much, too fast, and certainly too big," she said in a choked whisper. She had barely discovered she was falling in love with him, and now he was presenting her the most fantastic ring and asking for her hand.

"I understand that. This decision surprised me as well." Hope darkened his eyes. "How will you answer me, sweeting?"

Flutters moved through her belly from the endearment, but fear buzzed at the base of her spine. If she accepted the earl's proposal, her life would change exponentially and suddenly she would be vaulted into the position of countess. Everyone would look and her, gossip about her, scoff that a country nobody had landed an earl. Her hand shook in his while her heartbeat raced. The urge to retch grew strong as she stared. Terror filled her chest, for accepting his proposal meant she would be thrust into society.

Her throat went dry. Though she loved him, desperately wished to act upon that connection between them, her heart ached, for she would undoubtedly disappoint him, and he would grow to resent her for making such a large mistake as marrying her.

"Oh, Evan, I… I cannot do this." The whisper felt ripped from her throat. Quickly, she tore her hand from his hold, and as panic lanced down her spine, Christiana fled outside, onto the terrace through the French-paned doors.

For a handful of seconds, she marveled at the fact it was actually snowing but then she continued to run with no firm direction. Pelting into the winter-bare garden, she continued to run until a dead end on the path stymied her.

"Why is everything so confusing?"

The cold breeze didn't have the answers, and she shivered in the face of the temperature drop. Where to go now? As her mind spun, her heartbeat continued to race, and when the earl came into sight on the path, it pounded all the harder. He'd found her. Of course he did, for Evan was never far from her, even if it had only been four days since they were formally and properly introduced.

"Can I hope that you've run from me due to confusion and not because you are rejecting my offer?" Caution wove through his voice as he slowly approached her, and oh in his formal attire was so striking against the gently falling snowflakes.

"I don't know." At least it was honest.

"I can appreciate that." He came ever closer but paused with a few feet of space between them. "You are not the only one who has been at sixes and sevens because of love."

"Oh?" She gave into a shiver but couldn't help the curiosity from his words.

"Indeed." The earl tipped his head backward and stared into the midnight velvet sky. "Look. Just there." He pointed. "That bright star there isn't a star at all. It is, in fact, what they call the North Star, or the Christmas Star."

"I see it!" Even in the face of her potential refusal he would take the time to teach her about the heavens. It humbled her and left her heart aflutter.

"There are so many stars in our heavens, it would take a lifetime to discover them, to comb through them."

"I hope that you have that opportunity someday." She welcomed this aberration in conversation, for the sound of his voice brought her a modicum of calm.

"I aim to, especially if I have a good woman at my side." Even though he grinned, he made no move to close the distance. Once more, he stared into the darkened sky. "Coma Berenices is a collection of stars that cluster around the north galactic pole and is named after Queen Berenice II who ruled in Ancient Egypt between from 267-221 BC." As he warmed to his subject, his voice softened, and in profile while he grinned, he was most magnificent.

"Oh, dear. Is this a tragic story?"

Evan shrugged. "Only you can say by the end of it." His smile had her world tilting. "When Queen Berenice's husband Ptolemy III went to war, she was desperate to ensure his safe return."

"I can understand that. I would be beside myself with worry."

"Indeed." The look he sent her warmed her blood. "Her beautiful golden hair was the pride of Egypt, so she cut it off and laid the locks as a sacrifice in the temple of Aphrodite."

As he spoke, Christiana watched the heavens. Though it was snowing, there were still patches of clear sky as the breeze blew. "Was the offering accepted by Aphrodite?"

"It was." Then the earl shrugged out of his tailcoat and arranged it about her shoulders. The scent of him clung to the garment, and she breathed it in. "The goddess of love was so moved by Bernice's devotion that she delivered Ptolemy safely back to his wife and used the hair to decorate the sky in tribute to the lovers."

"What a lovely story."

"It truly is, and as the secrets of ancient Egypt are being uncovered, images of Queen Berenice have been discovered which show her with a shaved head."

"Then the stories are true?"

"Perhaps. Only those two lovers can say for certain."

"Oh." Unexpected tears filled her eyes. "That is so sad but also the height of romantic." But while he'd talked, her heartbeat had calmed, and her fears had begun to decline.

"Agreed. Although the Coma Berenices is faint, it is highly symbolic of the sacrifices made for love, and the power of the gods to protect those who seek protection."

"For the ones they adore the most," she said in a soft voice."

"Yes. The constellation circles the north pole much like the hair circled Queen Berenice's head, blessing us all with richness and beauty. So we will always remember just how deep love goes." For long moments, he remained silent. "I once told you that I would only believe in the magic of love at Christmastide if I saw snowflakes fly by Christmas Eve."

The hiss of snow falling around them strengthened his words. "What of it?" She wasn't of a mind for riddles and couldn't spare the strength to puzzle out his meaning.

"Oh, sweeting." His chuckle warmed her through. She didn't want to give into him, but he was so dear! "It's snowing, both outside and inside my ballroom." Such love twinkled in his eyes that she held her breath. "*You* made that happen for me before any of this started, and now that I believe in magic again—because you *are* that, by the way—I want to learn that trick for myself, but I cannot do it without you." Evan took her hand and threaded their fingers together. "Do you understand what I am saying?"

Trembles moved through her person. "You are merely swept away by the romance of the ball, the charm of it. Trying to woo me with tales of romance among the stars." She swallowed, but the dryness in her throat wasn't alleviated. "Once you come to your senses, you'll find this feeling isn't true, that it won't last."

Wouldn't he?

A frown tugged the corners of his mouth downward. "Is that what you have been telling yourself to explain away how *you* feel for *me*?"

Oh, dear. How could he possibly know her so well? "Am I that pathetic and transparent?" When he didn't answer, her cheeks heated. "I have been ignoring those feelings, actually."

"Why?"

A bit of panic spiraled through her chest, and she trembled harder. "Those feelings cannot possibly be real." Why had he given into fancy and she to logic?

"Poppycock. They are as real as I am, as real as the pressure of my fingers on yours." So saying, he squeezed her fingers.

As much as she wished to burrow into his arms and let him comfort her, she refrained and pulled his jacket tighter about her person. With a shake of her head, her spirits plummeted. "You should look elsewhere for a wife. One with a sterling pedigree. One who isn't terrified of the undertaking of such a position as you are asking me to fill. One who isn't a wallflower."

"But those are some of the very reasons why I love you." Easily, he tugged her into a loose embrace. "I'll be right there beside you."

"Not all the time."

"Of course not, but you will have my undying support, and little by little, you will grow in confidence and bravery just as our love grows. Perhaps as our family will grow," he added in a hushed voice as the snowflakes continued to fall.

The heat in her cheeks intensified. Flutters danced through her lower belly at the thought of having children with this man—a dream realized. But then she shook her head. "You must be foxed, Evan. This is madness." Yet her resolve to refuse him wavered. Could her thinking be flawed?

His chuckle provided a layer of encouragement. "Perhaps I am drunk on you, darling. And isn't love a form of madness? Shouldn't it be?" The earl released her hand only to cup her cheek and tilt her head back until their gazes connected. "It takes a bit of insanity to enter into it when you never know what will happen." That grin of his was so self-assured that she couldn't help but return it.

"You are impossible."

"Perhaps, but I'd rather think I am inevitable. That you and I were *always* meant for this moment. As if our story has been written in the stars, waiting for us to read it."

Oh, why was he so adorable? A giggle escaped her. "You won't stop trying to win me until you wear me down, will you?"

"I will not. It is, after all, just the beginning of Christmas Day, love. There are many more hours ahead to plead my case and cause. And I'm rather due a miracle." His fingers slid into her hair. "Don't let us suffer the same fate as Venus and Mars."

Her heart trembled, and she once more smiled. "I suppose I ought to accept, then."

"Oh? Why is that?" Such hope wove through his inquiry that her heart trembled.

There was no use denying it. "Because I'm hopelessly in love with you as well."

"Ah, Christiana. I have waited long to hear those words." His laugh of victory warmed her insides. Again, he presented her with the ring. "However, I am quite selfish and wish to hear you answer my question. Will you marry me?"

"Yes!" No longer did she feel the chill in the air. "I don't know how I ever thought I could refuse you. My life, my heart, is no longer my own now that I've met you."

"That is exactly how I feel as well. You are much like my North Star." Evan slipped the ring onto her finger, and it sparkled slightly in the dim light. He then caught her into his arms and claimed her lips with his.

As was always true with them, the embrace grew quickly out of hand. A growl came from him as he held her tighter and his jacket slipped from her shoulders, but she didn't care. Desire warmed her body, but love heated her heart. She now had a future to look forward to, and perhaps with him by her side, the remainder of her dreams would be realized.

Pulling away, she peered up at him with need tingling through every part of her. "Remember, though, I still wish to work with injured and sick animals. Please promise you will let me do that."

"Of course. None of those aspirations will change once we wed." Evan retrieved the jacket and put it once more about her shoulders. "But I have the means to make that happen easier for you, and I'm happy to do it, for you completely won me over with those snowflakes."

She patted his chest. "I merely wished for you to bring your heart out of hiding."

"How could I continue along that path when there was you waiting for me at the end?" He brushed his lips against hers. "Let us return to the house before you catch a head cold."

Eventually, they came into the library once more, where he pulled her down beside him on a low sofa before a cheerful fire in the hearth that had been lit while they were out. Had he planned on that? Of course he had, and he was such a dear. While they watched the fire, the muffled sounds of the string quartet and snatches of laughter from the ball down the corridor drifted to her ears. Christiana sighed with contentment and snuggled deeper into his embrace. She couldn't imagine how her future would look but she was excited to embrace it. The steady thud of the earl's heartbeat beneath her ear promised her all would be well.

"When will we marry? Do you wish to enjoy a long engagement?"

Evan snorted. He nuzzled her neck, and she nearly lost her train of thought. "I would say as soon as possible, for it we don't, I will almost certainly ruin you."

The heat had returned to her cheeks. "Is that so terrible, then? The idea sounds wonderful to me." To know the greatest intimacy with this man? *Oh, dear heavens.*

"Ah, Christiana." The earl held her tighter to his chest. "I adore your sense of humor." He chuckled as he kissed the top of her head. "Shall I procure a license so we might marry here? My mother was oddly enthusiastic about the match when I told her."

She snorted. "I somehow find that difficult to believe."

"Perhaps she thinks a bird in the hand, and all that."

"Then, yes. I would enjoy that very much. We can usher in a new year with our new life together."

Desire darkened his eyes to sapphire. "Practical as always."

"Oh, and I would like to take in a few dogs and cats."

"I would have been surprised if you did not. Stanton Hall is large enough. We shall even take some of them with us when we go down to London."

Flutters filled her belly at the thought. Finally, she would live in London and could see all the sights! "There is a sheep who is hobbled—"

He stopped her words with a searing kiss. "Let us start with the dogs and cats. At least until we're married and back from a wedding trip, hmm? Then you can start a clinic and take in all the animals you wish. Either here in Derbyshire or in London. It matters not to me as long as you are happy."

Another piece of her heart flew into his keeping. "You might regret those words, Stanton." Her mind still reeled over the fact she would soon marry this man.

"Never. Animals give you joy, and when you are joyful, you give me the same, and that has been a long time coming."

A sigh of contentment escaped her. "To think, you were my neighbor here in the country this whole time and I never knew my destiny lay so close." Thomas would be so very pleased she would marry an earl. "I should open my eyes and actually *see* more often."

"Perhaps we both should. And in my case, I apparently needed to see snowflakes on Christmas Eve."

"Or the light from the stars."

"Indeed." He held her even closer until she was nearly reclining on his lap. "There is so much I wish to show you, dearest, to teach you."

124

When he drew the pad of his thumb along her bottom lip, a shiver of need twisted down her spine. "We shall set aside time to watch the stars together…"

Her mind wandered as he spoke of various plans and hopes for the future. Perhaps having a man in her life wouldn't be the prison she'd once thought. Stepping into the unknown merely required belief in oneself… and a bit of Christmas magic didn't hurt either.

The End

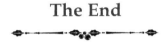

If you enjoyed this book, please leave a review on the site of your choice.

Regency-era romances by Sandra Sookoo

Willful Winterbournes series

Romancing Miss Quill
Pursuing Mr. Mattingly
Courting Lady Yeardly
Teasing Miss Atherby (coming February 2023)
Guarding the Widow Pellingham (coming May 2023)
Bedeviling Major Kenton (coming August 2023)
Charming Miss Standish (coming November 2023)

Singular Sensation series

One Little Indiscretion
One Secret Wish
One Tiny On-Dit Later (coming January 2023)
One Accidental Night with an Improper Duke (coming April 2023)
One Scandalous Choice (coming July 2023)
One Thing Led to Another (coming October 2023)
One Suitor Too Many (coming January 2024)
One of a Kind (as part of the *Gentleman and Gloves* anthology coming 2024)
One Track Mind (coming August 2024)
One Night in Covent Garden (coming October 2024)
One Christmas Disaster (coming December 2024)

Mary and Bright series

A Merry Little Crime Scene (a Mary and Bright mystery #1) (coming December 2023)
An Intriguing Springtime Engagement (a Mary and Bright mystery #2) (coming April 2024)
Autumn Means Marriage… and Murder (a Mary and Bright mystery #2) (coming October 2024)

Diamonds of London series

My Dear Mr. Ridley (coming March 2023)
The Widow's Daring Gambit (coming June 2023)
Catch Her if You Can (coming September 2023)
Magic for Christmas (coming December 2023)
When the Duke Said Yes (coming February 2024)
Along Came Tess (coming June 2024)
A Ghostly Affair (coming September 2024)
Spending Christmas in Hell (coming November 2024)
The Duke's Accidental Mistress (coming January 2025)
Only Spring will Do (coming March 2025)
Not in His Usual Style (coming May 2025)
The Duchess Problem (coming July 2025)
Kidnapped by a Rogue (coming September 2025)
A Bit of Christmas Fiction (coming November 2025)
If a Spinster Wishes (coming January 2026)

Disreputable Dukes of Club Damnation

Ravenhurst's Return (coming November 2024)
His by Sunrise (coming February 2025)
Promised to the Worst Duke in England (coming April 2025)
The Devil's in the Details (coming June 2025)
The Duchess' Damning Secret (coming August 2025)
Buckthorne's Secret (coming October 2025)
A Duchess for Christmas (coming December 2025)
In Hell by Default (coming February 2026)

Colors of Scandal series

Dressed in White
Draped in Green
Trimmed in Blue
Wrapped in Red
Graced in Scarlet
Adorned in Violet
Embellished in Mauve
Clad in Midnight
Garbed in Purple
Resplendent in Ruby
Cloaked in Shadows
Decorated in Christmas
Tangled in Lavender

Persuasive in Pink
Disguised in Tartan
Attired in Highland Gold
Hopeful in Yellow
Imperfect in Peridot
Christmas in Crimson
Outrageous in Orchid (coming November 2023 as part of the *Earls and Pearls* anthology)

Storme Brothers series

The Soul of a Storme
The Heart of a Storme
The Look of a Storme
A Storme's Christmas Legacy
A Storme's First Noelle
The Sting of a Storme
The Touch of a Storme
The Fury of a Storme
Much Ado About a Storme (as part of the *Duke in Winter* anthology)

Standalone Regency romances

Lady Isabella's Splendid Folly
Wagering on Christmas
Magic in Mayflowers
Act of Pardon
Angel's Master
Storm Tossed Rogue
Claiming His Wife
Scoundrel's Trespass
On a Midnight Clear
A Fowl Christmastide
His Pretend Duchess
Visions of Christmastide
The Viscount's Bluestocking Vixen
An Accidental Countess
A Rogue for Lady Peacock
The Most Wonderful Earl of the Year
Snowflakes for an Earl
She's Got a Duke to Keep Her Warm

The Lyon's Puzzle (Lyon's Den connected world) (coming January 2023)
Duchess of Moonlight (TBA 2023)
She's in Love with the EArl (TBA 2023)
The Lyon's Secret (Lyon's Den connected world) (coming October 2023)

Author Bio

Sandra Sookoo is a *USA Today* bestselling author who firmly believes every person deserves acceptance and a happy ending. She's written for publication since 2008. Most days you can find her creating scandal and mischief in the Regency-era, serendipity and happenstance in the Victorian era, or historical romantic suspense complete with mystery and intrigue. Reading is a lot like eating chocolates—you can't just have one book. Good thing they don't have calories!

When she's not wearing out computer keyboards, Sandra spends time with her real-life Prince Charming in Central Indiana where she's been known to bake cookies and make moments count because the key to life is laughter. A Disney fan since the age of ten, when her soul gets bogged down and her imagination flags, a trip to Walt Disney World is in order. Nothing fuels her dreams more than the land of eternal happy endings, hope and love stories.

Stay in Touch

Sign up for Sandra's bi-monthly newsletter and you'll be given exclusive excerpts, cover reveals before the general public as well as opportunities to enter contests you won't find anywhere else.

Just send an email to sandrasookoo@yahoo.com with SUBSCRIBE in the subject line.

Or follow/friend her on social media:

Facebook: https://www.facebook.com/sandra.sookoo

Facebook Author Page:
https://www.facebook.com/sandrasookooauthor/

Pinterest: https://www.pinterest.com/sandrasookoo/

Instagram: https://www.instagram.com/sandrasookoo/

BookBub Page:
https://www.bookbub.com/authors/sandra-sookoo

Website: http://www.sandrasookoo.com

Also, if you want to join my ARC review team on BookSprout, here's the link:
https://booksprout.co/reviewer/team/10540/sandra-sookoos-review-team Bear in mind, these ARCS go fast, like in a few hours the day I post so make sure you're signed up for notifications.

Made in the USA
Monee, IL
10 December 2022

20727689R00077